Dedicate
My Author Assistant Emily

ME: What do you want for your birthday?

EMILY: A Russian Mafia Romance!!

ME: Really? 🤔

EMILY: Hardcore Alpha. A boss of all bosses. Slow burn love. No insta-love. Super sexy.

ME: Ok, but it's going to be a mindfuck until the end.

Emily:

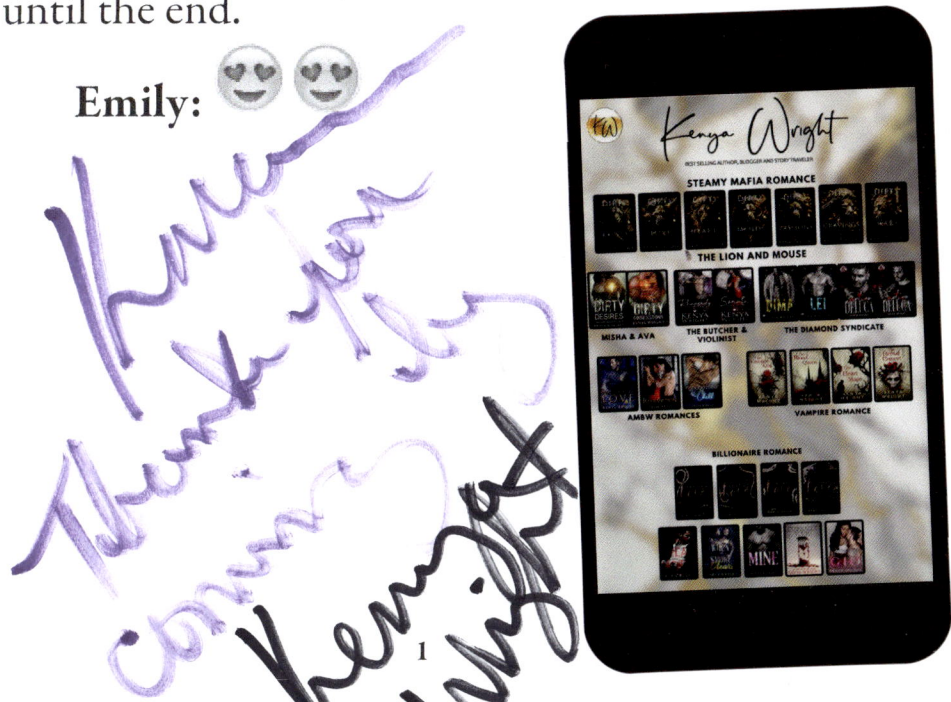

Happy Birthday, Emily!

"The world
is a dangerous place to live
not because of the people
who are evil,
but because of the people
who don't
do anything about it."
— Albert Einstein

Act One

Definition of Dirty

1: morally unclean or corrupt.
dirty players
dirty games

Prologue
Kazimir

Rumi is dead. Who did it?

Rumi was born with both sexual organs. He liked to brag that he had a big clitoris and penis. That wasn't why someone killed him, but it was the most interesting thing about him. And I hadn't flown to New York because I cared about him. He cleaned my money in America, so whoever murdered Rumi was messing with me.

Who killed him?

Every country spawned criminals—poor people with nothing to lose, fighting the world to survive, willing to do anything. Kill. Rob. Traffic. America birthed outlaws—Jesse James to the Hell's Angels, Bloods to the Crips. Italians not only perfected pasta, they bred the *men of honor*—the Mafia, Mob, *La Cosa Nostra*. China gave us Triads. Then, there was the Corsicon in France, Mexico's drug cartels, and the full-body tattooed Yakuza in Japan.

Poor people with nothing to lose. Because the country had taken it from them. Because some societies gave to the rich and bled the poor. Because sometimes evil was necessary and blood should be spilled and money lured the pure into dirty, filthy things.

Most of the time, souls shattered in poverty.

In Russia, we had the *Bratva*—the brotherhood. And when someone of this time wrote about the brotherhood, they mentioned me, often dedicating chapters on my life.

New Yorkers should read more, before I level this state down to dirt and dead bodies.

My limo turned onto Furman Street in a posh area of Brooklyn.

My step brother Sasha sat on my right. After his mother died, his father married his mistress—my mother. We'd had a rough beginning but eventually learned to love each other.

They'd called his father the King. Long ago, he'd been *Vory v Zakone*—a thief in law. Later, he ran Bratva and was killed.

By all accounts, my step brother Sasha should've been the next in line, but I'd gained too much of a reputation by the time of his father's death. And there was the problem of Sasha enjoying the pleasure of men. The Bratva was trenched in old thinking.

Nevertheless, I loved Sasha.

Many called him the wolf. Within the shadows on a snowy night, he resembled one. His pale blond hair was cut close to his head. He'd received slanted, exotic eyes from his mother.

Although I was dark haired, many thought we were brothers. We both had large frames and broad shoulders.

Sasha turned to me. "This is dangerous, Kazimir. Talk to the witness. Don't kill him."

"Someone murdered my top washer in America," I said. "Sliced him from ear-to-ear and wrapped his intestines around his neck. And even worse they took my fifty million dollars with them."

"You shouldn't even be in the United States right now."

Sasha was correct, but I'd sniffed out blood and was too excited to be careful. Unfortunately for the killer, I'd been in Toronto for my niece's christening. Little Natalya was my first niece out of five rambunctious nephews. She was more than worth a visit, regardless of Interpol and the FBI. Had I been in Russia, when they killed Rumi, I would've never made it in time.

Sasha decided to push the point further. "With this immigration nonsense and their suspicions of Trump-Russian election tampering, they'll have their eyes everywhere."

"America's too busy bullying Muslim families to keep up with me."

"They're watching *everyone*," he said.

"If you believe that, then you haven't been paying attention."

"I'm just—"

"I stay in New York, until everything is solved."

Sasha muttered under his breath, "*Idiota kusok.*"

Only my brother could call me a piece of an idiot and not die.

A man's status in the upper ranks of Bratva was measured by several factors—the total of men he killed, the amount of countries that feared him, and his ranking on the FBI's Most wanted list. By those measures, one could argue that I was a very important man. I had over two hundred kills, was restricted from entering the Americas and most of Western Europe, and by the age of twenty the FBI had placed me at #490 on the most wanted list—ten steps from Usama Bin Laden.

I was now thirty.

I'd outlived Bin Laden, moved up the Most Wanted list, and headed Bratva.

The limo stopped in front of an upscale building where my dead washer now lay in his penthouse. My men held a possible suspect, waiting for my arrival.

"Kazimir." Sasha turned to me. "You should fear this country."

"Fear is an illusion. The only way fear can breathe, is in our thoughts of the future." I touched the side of my head. "We choose fear. But, it's a product of our imagination. Not our reality."

"Fear can be rational," he countered.

"Sure, when the bear is in front of a man standing on a mountain, he fears the beast and jumps into action. But the problem with humanity is that the man fears the bear right before he even goes to the mountain. Thus, never climbing up. The man stays where he is. He hides, and he says to himself, I'm safe because the bear is on the mountain. But what if the bear is right behind him?"

"*Mne vse ravno,*" Sasha muttered, "I don't care about your damn bear, I want you safe."

"You put too much value in this country. America is neither a bear or a mountain."

"Nevertheless," Sasha climbed out of the limo. "I could've handled this."

I followed. "I like New York."

"No, you don't. You came because you don't trust me to get back the money and find the one responsible. You never trust me."

Because you always fuck it up, and people only respect you, because they're afraid of me.

I thought back to an argument I had with my sister days earlier.

"You should wait a few days, and then I can come with you," my sister Valentina said.

"No." I held my niece. "Spend time with your daughter. You never get a rest with our world."

"I don't like Rumi being murdered. It makes me nervous."

"Everything will be fine." I handed back my sleeping niece to Valentina. "Keep my niece safe. We have too many men in our family. We need more women."

Already I missed my niece.

It was odd that something so small as a newborn baby, could capture my attention and make me leave Russia. The years had passed. I'd lost count of the days. The sun became the moon, and then the moon became the sun. Money and power had come. And yet when I turned thirty, I wondered what else I would do with my life.

What else is there in life?

I paused and looked up at the night sky, barely able to see it with all the tall buildings. "It's a full moon tonight. They say it's a super moon."

Sasha snorted. "Must we talk about your moon?"

"Everything is connected."

"It always is with you."

"The Moon, Earth, and Sun are aligned," I said. "There's a major gravitational pull happening. That's why there are tides in the oceans, when there's a full moon."

"So, this isn't a good time to fish?"

"Or kill," I admitted.

Sasha raised his eyebrows. "Why?"

"If the moon can move the ocean, surely it can move us. We're 75% water."

"Then, good. We don't need to kill this guy. Keep him alive."

Our conversation ended as two men walked up to me. They didn't need uniforms. I could smell the *politsiya* all over them.

Plain clothes NYPD.

Fortunately, they were also my cops—on the New York payroll. They handed my brothers information, when necessary. They destroyed evidence and cases, when required.

Both men appeared uncomfortable. One kept checking over his shoulders as if hoping his fellow brothers in blue wouldn't catch him working with the enemy. The other looked young, probably early twenties. He held his stomach with both hands like he'd just ate bad uncooked meat and was close to doubling over.

I turned to Mr. Nervous. "What do you have for me?"

"A coroner friend owed me a favor and looked it over. Rumi died last night from blood lost. Mainly from all the stab wounds to his groin. There weren't many fingerprints where they killed Rumi or security, but we grabbed something. The photos of the scene are with your men upstairs." The nervous one checked over his shoulder again. "I might have a lead."

Sasha inched forward.

Mr. Nervous pulled out a small note pad and flipped it open. "Rumi was a top customer with a high-end brothel in SoHo managed by a Penelope Fairchild. My understanding is that this one is affiliated with your. . .organization."

Sasha nodded.

"Good," I said. "We'll go talk to this Penelope later."

Mr. Nervous continued, "Rumi had a woman delivered every night at ten pm from the brothel. The madam Penelope had a key to his place that she gave to the girls, so they could just let themselves in, go to his bedroom, and pleasure him."

He always was a lazy bastard.

The cop read on, "The girls were always eighteen or older, but Rumi liked them to look young. Tonight, he didn't cancel. Penelope sent the girl in a limo. According to the limo driver, the girl went into the building and phoned that she was in the condo. Two hours passed. She never came out. The limo driver was the one that found the body. Rumi's door was opened and the girl had disappeared."

A dead washer and a missing hooker. New York is always full of surprises.

"Anything else?" I asked.

"As far as finding prints or the killer's DNA, the clean-up job was professional. I doubt I'll have something. The killer took the footage and somehow bypassed the building's high-tech security. But the murder...I don't think it's..." Mr. Nervous lowered his voice. "I don't think it's mafia related. This looks emotional. The stabbing was done with rage. Jagged and very messy. What the person did to his...private area was brutal."

The young one holding his stomach spoke up, "Sick. The intestines...and...smiley faces."

He doubled over and vomited a little onto the sidewalk.

Sasha frowned.

We walked a few feet away.

Mr. Nervous shook his head. "Sorry. He's new to shit like this."

I kept my gaze on Mr. Nervous. "Smiley faces?"

"For some reason the person drew smiley faces all over Rumi's legs. I don't know what it means. I'm doing a search to see, if other victims were found this way. We've already got a psycho running around the city killing men in hotels. We're calling him the Tinder Killer. What we don't need is another serial killer in Manhattan."

"Let me know anything else you find." I walked off.

The young cop continued to retch behind us.

"Maybe you're right about the full moon and its effect on people." Sasha followed. "The tide was definitely working with that one."

"Not everybody's made for this." I entered the building.

Our armed men led the way. Silence filled the elevator as it took us up.

I turned to Sasha. Fear radiated off him. It was subtle, but I'd known him all my life. He wore a neutral expression—the one I called the mask. It covered his face—gaze straight, the mouth barely formed into a line, no movement in his shoulders as usual.

"What's wrong?" I asked.

He continued to stare at the door. "You're being reckless."

I smiled. "The world belongs to the bold."

Sasha said nothing.

Chapter 1
Kazimir

The elevator doors slid open to Rumi's stunning loft. It had floor-to-ceiling windows showing off endless water and sky views. I made out the Empire State building off in the distance. We turned right into a ballroom-sized formal living room with an adjacent casual office.

Paintings of naked angels decorated the walls, but these angels were young girls. Barely developed. Budding breasts and hairless vaginas. My stomach twisted as we moved on.

They said Rumi was a pervert. Was he the disgusting type?

The Bratva didn't have many rules, but many frowned on homosexuality and pedophilia. And when the Bratva frowned, many died.

"I don't think it's mafia related," the cop had said. *"This looks emotional."*

I didn't care about a man being gay, but I enjoyed killing molesters. If Rumi had been a pedophile, lucky for him. He'd hid it well. If I'd known, I would've done more than intestines and smiley faces.

On the left, there was an enormous kitchen near a formal dining room that could seat about twenty people.

In every country, I kept my washer in an upscale place. They had to play the part of the rich while cleaning my dirty money. Of course, I owned the property and kept it monitored by cameras and round-the-clock personal security.

Rumi's security guy was an ex-NY cop.

We walked to the back, found the security room, and stepped inside.

The police had done a lousy job with clearing the area. Blood stains remained.

One of my men covered his nose from the stench and handed me a folder of photos. "This is what the guy did to the security person and Rumi."

I opened the folder. "Interesting."

In the photos, the cop floated in a pool of his own blood. A burnt-out cigarette rested between his cold, stiff lips.

I checked the images of Rumi.

He lay on the floor. There was a bloody smile cut into his face and tattered with pink ripped flesh at the corners of his neck. A cross was carved into his chest. His intestines were wrapped around his neck. The other end of the slimy length was still attached to the inside of his gut. His eyes had been frozen open in shock. There'd been more knife wounds on his chest. And as the cops told us, tons of smiley faces were drawn in blood, all over his legs.

But what the person did to his groin. . .even *I* found it difficult to look at.

"These stabs aren't precise. They're crazy. All over the place. More jabs." I pointed to one of the wounds, showing Sasha. "Look at that. With a sharp blade and with precision, it would've just been a line and scarring with blood leaking out. This one has the flesh yanked out. It's almost like two people did it."

Sasha rolled his eyes. "Probably a hook knife too, and what are you doing. . .investigating?"

I ignored the comment. "Where's Rumi?"

My men took me down the hall. Hundreds of dildos and cracked wine bottles covered the floor as if someone had scattered them around. Shelves were slung on their sides. It looked like an orgy that had gone bad.

One of my men pointed to the room. "This way, sir."

I stepped over the dildos. Many of them were two to three feet long. I couldn't imagine any women enjoying them.

Did you like them, Rumi?

Sasha and I entered the room. A large tube of lube sat on his office desk. A leather suit rested on the chair.

Sasha grinned. "A man after my own heart."

That's the other reason why I'm doing this myself. You have no discipline.

I walked to the other side of the desk.

Sasha remained where he was, studying the leather.

"The killer had no control." I looked up at one of my men and asked in Russian. "Did you find anything?"

"Just a wig under the desk," he replied. "Everything was wiped pretty clean, but we'll keeping looking. We'll find something."

"Where's the guy who should have answers?" I asked.

"In the game room." They led the way.

I followed. "Good. I've always been a fan of games."

I walked into the room and stood in front of a crumbled man—beat up by life, beat up by my men. Brown skin. Bald head. Lots of muscle. Probably could've been a boxer or a football player had anyone cared about him.

With some people, childhood pain raged within the eyes, settling at the core of angry pupils. He had those eyes. He'd probably been unlucky since the day he was born.

The fact that I stood in front of him meant his luck wouldn't improve.

I took off my jacket, unbuttoned my shirt, and shed that too. One of my men grabbed them. Although I wasn't a fashion person like my sister Valentina—always needing to buy this designer or that—I hated blood on my suit.

I gestured to my men. "Lift his head."

They did.

Blood streamed down his face as he coughed and spat out murky saliva. He blinked his bruised eyes and squinted at me, probably taking in the tattoo on my bare arm.

It was a lion climbing up a rocky cliff. The huge creature's mane waved in the air. His eyes roared fiercely violent. His claws looked so sharp against my skin many women told me they feared they'd be cut from caressing the bicep.

My brother walked in, spotted the beaten guy, and frowned. "Next time, clean this up before you call us."

My men nodded.

Sasha hated blood—the scent, the feel, the sight. Even when he killed, he did so in clean ways—ropes, needles, drowning, etc. Our other brothers joked that he murdered like an old woman. Always hanging this person or that.

"It's messy." Sasha looked away and probably would continue to avoid the scene.

I took off my watch, pocketed it, and turned to the beaten guy. "What's your name?"

"Darryl." Blood dripped from the corner of his lip. "I told them. I-I don't who did it. I don't know how to do what he did. I can't—"

I shrugged. "Then, are you ready to die, Darryl?"

"No! Please, God no."

"I need a solution." I walked over to him.

"I don't know who did it! I don't!" Darryl scrambled back, struggling to get out of my men's hold.

Fifty million dollars is missing. You're lucky your heart is still beating and none of your legs are broken.

In a calm voice, I asked, "Where's my money?"

"I-I don't know. I—"

"Relax." I stopped in front of him and kneeled to face him. "Do you know who I am?"

Darryl shivered and nodded his head. "You're the Russian Lion."

"You silly Americans." I smiled. "I am not *the Russian* lion." I leaned in closer. "I am the Lion, and there are no others above or on my level."

"Y-yes, s-sir."

"It's always important to know who you're having a conversation with. Don't you agree?"

"Y-yes." Darryl's chest rose and fell like he'd been running.

"Let's begin." I gestured at my men.

They let Darryl go. He dropped to the floor.

One of my men brought me over a chair. I rose and sat in it. Darryl stared at me, trembling with my every movement.

A man pushed over a tray full of beautiful things—fire torch, several different hand saws, a trusty hammer, pliers, a cheese grater, and nail gun. I studied the tray wondering what I would start with first.

"Do not use the cheese grater." Sasha glanced at the tray. "I hate, when you do it."

I shrugged at Darryl. "My brother doesn't have the stomach for certain things."

Darryl pissed his pants, staining his jeans. Urine spilled out on the carpet under him.

"Fine. No cheese grater this evening." I grabbed the nail gun, leaned back in my chair, crossed my legs, and rested the gun on my lap. "Do you know a lot about lions, Darryl?"

He stared at the nail gun, his lip quivering with each second. "N-no."

"Although they are the largest animals, lions are not the best hunters." I trailed the length of the nail gun with my thumb. "Lions survive because they hunt in groups. Loyalty is important. And they're hunting methods are ruthless and scientific."

I gestured for him to come closer.

Darryl crawled my way, reeking of urine. When he got a few inches from me, he placed his hands into a praying position. "P-please—"

"Do you know why they call me the Lion?"

"N-no, sir."

"A lion's favorite way to kill is suffocation." I rushed for him, wrapped one hand around his throat, and placed the tip of the nail gun to his temple.

My movement caught everyone by surprise. Darryl screamed before finding himself choked. My men grabbed their guns not knowing what was going on and then quickly put them away.

I stared into Darryl's eyes as he struggled against choking. "They call me the Lion because I'm fast, when I attack. At times, I surprise myself."

Sasha turned our way and took out a cigarette. "Really, Kazimir? There's no need for you to get dirty."

Darryl struggled, clawing at my hands and fighting to breathe.

I tightened my hold on his windpipe and turned to Sasha. "Come on, brother. I never get blood on my hands anymore."

"Respectfully, I believe we don't have the time. If Rumi was meant to hurt our money, then there will be a war to deal with. You'll have plenty of time for blood." Sasha lit his cigarette, inhaled, and blew out a circle. "Maybe, we should ask him questions. Instead of choke him."

"I'm getting to that. This is foreplay." I let go of Darryl's throat and slung him to the floor. "Ignore my brother. He's always in a bad mood, when he comes to America. You can't get a good vodka here."

Darryl coughed into his hands as he lay on the floor.

"But enough about my brother." I kneeled by Darryl. "Here's an interesting fact. A single lion will often get a good bite on its victim's throat and crush the windpipe." I brought the nail gun to his face and pressed the tip on his temple.

"P-please, I don't know anything."

"While that lion is suffocating the prey, it is not odd for the other lions to open the abdomen." I moved the nail gun to his stomach. "And then the lions will begin eating while the animal is still being suffocated."

Darryl jerked away from the gun.

"So, tell me, Darryl. Why do you think they call me the lion?"

"B-because. . .you're f-fast, ruthless, and smart and. . .you kill—"

"Good job." I patted his head and walked back to my chair. "That was fun, but we should stop playing and get down to business. Do you know Alana?"

"Yes."

"You fucked her this morning, right after Rumi died?" I asked.

"Yes."

"And you told her that you washed money for Rumi. Millions of dollars. You said you had a plan in the works where you would be running New York." I tapped the nail gun on my lap. "This is good for me because if you don't have anything to do with Rumi's murder, then you can take over his washing. It seems a position is open."

Darryl scrambled back to his knees and did that praying motion again. "Y-yes, but I was just telling her that to fuck, not to—"

"Remember, Darryl. Lions hunt in groups. She's a scout."

"I lied. It was all to impress her."

"But, you do work for Rumi?"

"Yes, but I'm low level. I'm no one."

"Your name is on every property he owns."

"It's just a front. It's to. . ." Darryl shook his head in defeat. "It's just a front to clean his money."

"But, you said you're low level."

Sasha tapped ash on the floor. "Darryl, perhaps you should get to explaining the situation quickly, before my brother gets angry."

Darryl wiped his face with his shaking fingers. "Okay. Okay. Back in the day, before Rumi got up with yall. Someone cleaned the money for Rumi. She taught him how to do it."

"Why?"

"Because Rumi and I had. . .a problem, but I was working with him. She put my name on everything."

I raised my eyebrows. "Why?"

"To keep me safe. If I'm on all of Rumi's shit, then he probably would think twice before killing me. But that was years ago, before he got this big. All the money washing shit. I don't know nothing about it."

"You're not saving yourself." I gripped the nail gun. "I have no reason to keep you alive. You don't know who killed Rumi. You don't know where my money is, and you have no idea how to clean."

"Who was the woman who started Rumi off? Whoever taught Rumi was flawless." Sasha finished his cigarette, put it on the ground, and stomped it out with his foot. "I saw Rumi's financial records. Every damn penny was sparkling clean from the very first day. There was a clear system in place. Maybe, you should introduce us to this person. They're efficient and can clearly keep their mouth closed."

"But. . ." Darryl rubbed his face again and this time he looked more scared than ever. "It's my sister, man. I can't do that to her."

"Where is she?" I asked.

He didn't say anything.

I rose from my seat.

Perhaps, Darryl thought I would ask him the question again with more sternness. Maybe even throw in a threat and glare at him.

I'd become bored. There was no need for words, unless they gave a name and location. Until then, we would talk with blood.

I shot a nail into his upper thigh.

"No!" Darryl rolled away. "Fuck! My sister's name is Emily. She's in Harlem."

Blood dripped from his leg. His whole body shook as he screamed in pain.

I tapped the gun against his other leg. "I need more information, Darryl."

"S-she has an art showing today. Her paintings. S-she has a gallery." Tears spilled out of his eyes. "I can show you. I-I can take you there."

"Hmmm." I began to shoot him again.

Sasha placed his hand on my shoulder. "We've got the information."

"Yes, but once I start, I like to—"

"This is why we don't let you get dirty anymore." Sasha gestured for our men to get Darryl. "Let's clean up. We have an art event to go to."

I didn't rise yet.

Sasha looked at Darryl. "Is your sister any good?"

"Huh?" Darryl shook on the ground, glancing back and forth from Sasha to me.

"Is your sister a good painter?" Sasha asked.

"I've never seen Emily lose at anything," Darryl whispered.

I wiped my nail gun on Darryl's pants. "Then, let's hope your sister's luck is better than yours."

Sasha walked off and handed out orders to our men. "Get the address and take us over."

I got to my brother's side. "A woman washer?"

Sasha nodded. "I'm sure it's not odd for others."

I set the nail gun on Rumi's desk and then we left the penthouse, bypassing blood, death, and scattered dildos.

When we got outside, I said, "I hope Darryl's sister is smarter than her brother. I hate killing women."

Sasha laughed. "It's because you're too busy trying to fuck them."

"That's what they're here for."

"No. One day you'll meet a woman who will change that thinking."

I paused in front of the elevator and gave Sasha the oddest look. "Do you really think those?"

The elevator arrived. The doors opened.

Sasha laughed again. "No. I don't. I just like to sound human every now and then."

I shook my head. "Being human is so boring."

"Yes. Yes." Sasha walked on the elevator. "It's nothing as exciting as being a lion."

I thought back to that conversation with Darryl. "Too bad I didn't get to use the blow torch."

"There is that." Sasha gestured for me to come on. "I'm sure there will be more opportunities."

I walked on the elevator. "We'll go see this Emily. She does what we want, we leave New York. If she does not, then we kill her in front of Darryl and have him see if he can find someone else."

Sasha added, "And hopefully we'll buy a nice painting or two."

"There is that."

Chapter 2
Emily

I had another blackout. This one was worse than the others. This morning, I woke up in my office in strange clothes. My pocketbook hadn't disappeared. My phone and wallet lay inside. I still had on my gold heart locket.

My stomach twisted.

Whatever guy I'd met had the good grace to not rob or hurt me.

But then why did he change my clothes? And how did I end up back in my office? I can't believe I fucking blacked out.

A voice sounded in front of me. "Emily?"

There'd been money in the desk. The stranger hadn't even looked. Maybe I'd drunkenly told the person to bring me here. I made a point to never bring anyone home. At least, I had it together enough to not do that.

"Emily?"

I looked up from my desk.

"Emily, are you okay?" My best friend Kennedy stood in my office's doorway.

Those bouncy corkscrew curls outlined her face. Kennedy had that mixed look where people never knew exactly what she was. Some said Dominican. Others guessed black and white. I knew it was black and Japanese.

I, on the other hand, looked African American. Brown skin and a huge kinky afro that I barely brought out. Tonight, I kept it braded and hidden under my favorite wig.

I loved my hair but had a special addiction to wigs. They let me hide and pretend. Back in my brownstone I had tons of wigs. Wigs for partying. Wigs for fucking. Wigs for adventure. All brushed and pampered, used and then placed back in my closet like museum pieces.

I'd given each wig a name.

Tonight, I wore Cynthia. She was long silky strands of ebony that passed my shoulders.

Kennedy walked in and towered over me.

I was short next to her.

She could've been a model. We'd both dreamed of it, when we were kids playing with our dolls. She ended up growing tall and slim—perfect for a runway. I resulted in short and super curvy due to my mom's voluptuous DNA. One look at my hips and breasts and a fashion agency would suggest I do porn instead of glamour magazines.

Kennedy pointed at my wig. "I see you're wearing Cynthia today."

Smiling, I shook my hair. "This is my art debut. Cynthia had to come out."

There was one thing that I learned in life. I needed different identities to survive. Compartments. Alter egos. My Cynthia look came out to play, when I was super nervous. She was all sleek and sexy business attire. Fitted, designer clothes. Heels that cost more than most people's rent.

"Why have you been sitting in here the whole time?" Kennedy stepped inside and closed the office door. "We've started. The gallery is filling up. What are you doing?"

I blinked. "Everyone's already here?"

"Uh, yeah." She flashed her watch at me. "It's been an hour. What's going on?"

Damn it. I thought it was morning. What's going on?

"Nothing." I rose. "I just partied too much last night."

"I'm glad you ended up having fun. You were pissed, when you left, cursing and looking through your Tinder."

I scanned my brain trying to remember yesterday. "I was mad last night?"

"Yeah. Something about someone trying to cock block your evening. Anyway, I'm glad you ended up enjoying yourself." She grinned. "What hot Tinder guy did you hook up with? Let me guess. He had some stupid name like Baby2U or BrickCity69?"

I frowned. "I can't remember."

"Again?" She widened her eyes in shock. "Girl, you need to chill on the drinking. You know there's a serial killer out there."

"Yeah. The Tinder Killer, but he's killing guys."

"Doesn't matter."

"I know. I know." An ache beat at my head. I grabbed my water bottle, finished it, and headed out of the office. "I'm done with alcohol."

"You said that shit two days ago."

"I just turned twenty-one. Give me a break. It's like a rite of passage to be drunk the whole year."

"Yeah, but you've been drinking since we were kids."

I had no response.

"At least work on getting the sex thing fixed." She followed me down the hall. "I worry about you."

The sex thing fixed?

I didn't comment again. I loved her, but she was the type of friend to act like a judgmental mother, always nagging and questioning. Granted, she cared for me with every inch of her heart. Due to that, she could say what she wanted.

She probably has a point anyway. I just don't want to deal with my mess.

"You know what?" Kennedy shook her head. "Who am I to judge?"

"No." I let out a long breath. "You're right. I do need to work on it."

Chatter and soft giggling sounded ahead of us.

We entered the main gallery.

People crowded the place. Jazz music filled the space and rose against the chatter. Glasses clinked. Kennedy had dimmed the lights to keep the focus on the art.

All my paintings had a cordless picture light mounted at the top of their frames, casting a warm white glow over the works. Twelve large beasts covered the wall. All of them were lions, clawing and roaring, hunting and attacking. There were a few paintings that showed the lions' calmer life—a lioness licking her cubs, a lion lounging on the top of a cliff as wind blew through his hair. They were all mixed media images—paint and tiny crystals that took me forever to place in the right places.

My stomach calmed.

This exposé could lead to more opportunities—and they would be legal ones. I wouldn't have to hid what I did, and they wouldn't be so dangerous.

This is going to help us.

I drank in the area.

Beautifully dressed couples browsing the paintings. Many of them held hands. Groups of women strolled around along with a good bit of men. They all nibbled on the hors d'euvres.

Kennedy stood on my side and softly tapped my arm. "I'm just saying. Maybe you should get a long-term guy instead of doing one-night stands, when you're horny."

Girl, are we still on that?

I nodded and walked away, needing to get lost in the buzzing energy of those around me.

Kennedy might've had a point, but we were different when it came to men. She needed their love and attention, damn near survived on it more than food and water. I just wanted their dicks, every now and then. They could keep the rest of their bullshit to themselves.

I was introduced to sex too young. Too wrong.

By the time, I was old enough to love, my heart was a little bag of poisonous fear. Paralyzing fear. Fear of love. Fear of men. Fear of them getting too close. Fear of them seeing invisible bruises.

"Girl, I told you I could introduce you to some nice guys in my classes."

"I'm good."

Kennedy gazed around. "Do you think Darryl arrived yet?"

"Nope." I rolled my eyes at the mention of my brother. "I doubt he's here. I don't hear the cops or any other signs of trouble."

"You're so hard on me."

That's one way to look at it.

Darryl kept me in trouble. It was normal for me—my cross to bear.

But I wasn't a fan of how he treated my best friend. He should've never started dating Kennedy, when we were teens. Since then, they'd been off and on forever. They were a never-ending cycle of dysfunction—he fucked around, and she waited until he got bored and returned to her. In these recent years, she'd taken on a maternal role, closing her eyes to all his sexual adventures, yet always being his *ride or die chick*—as if that even meant anything to him.

It didn't matter, if there was video footage of Darryl sleeping with another woman broadcasting in Times Square, he would dance his way out of it. And he was a ballerina, when it came to escaping break ups. He could plie and releve with the best of them, but the true skill was in his leaps over reality and the ways he was able to balance himself on the tightrope of delusion.

Basically, if he hadn't been my brother, I would've cut his penis for what he'd done to her.

"I'm going to call Darryl and see if he's on his way." Kennedy rushed off without my response.

It might be better, if Darryl stays over whatever chick he's found this evening. Then he could keep his butt out of trouble.

I passed by a couple talking about my art.

"Extraordinary." The man pointed to the painting and gestured toward the lion on the canvas. "I've never seen a more astonishing creature. The use of light and shadow. The mixed media."

The woman with him nodded. "I feel like the lion is going to jump off the canvas and rip my head off."

I walked further down and neared a critic. I'd seen him at other artists' showings. I was happy he'd showed up at mine.

He spoke into his phone, probably using a recorder app to gather his notes. "...Emily is one of the youngest artists to be included in the Met's new modern art collection celebrating Harlem."

Yes! He's doing an article on me. I hope it's good. Shit. It doesn't matter. He's talking about me. That's good enough.

My other bestie Maxwell stood back from the group of exhibit attendees, nursing a flute of champagne and surrounded by gorgeous women. He'd take one or two home this evening.

Maxwell had those panty-dropping looks. Light brown skin. Hazel eyes. Tall, with a body to die for. Huge arms and a rock-hard chest. To most, Maxwell was hot. But for me, we remained in the friend zone.

We shared too many dark memories. Loving each other wouldn't wash the filth away. And even if we didn't share a haunted past, Maxwell was a man-whore after all.

Not that I was an angel either.

What happened last night? Just forget about it for now. Enjoy the moment.

I walked around, doing my best not to creep anybody out as I listened in on conversations. Many were enthused over the dozen large paintings displayed on the gallery walls. Others tried to guess why I'd chosen a lion as my subject matter.

A man with huge glasses on his head spoke to a group of four. "The lion must symbolize Africa and her journey back to her roots. Do you see how the shape of this lion's pupils are the shape of the African continent?"

Wow. They are? That damn sure wasn't intentional, but I'll take that.

"Yes. Yes." The women next to him nodded. "I see. Remarkable. Tribal. I can hear Mother Africa humming."

The others nodded.

The man with the glasses continued, "She's telling us that we can never forget our heritage, no matter how much it was ripped away from us and covered in blood."

Really? It's just a lion on a cliff about to take a nap.

I continued toward the center and caught more conversation.

"This is so erotic." A man held the hand of another. Both men were tall.

The other kissed his cheek. "We have to get this one. It's all about independence from the social constraints that society puts on sexuality."

"Tell me about it." He gestured to the lion's long, thick tail. "And that is an obvious phallic symbol. This would go great in the dining room. Sexual, but not overt."

I was glad no one stopped me to ask about the art. I was still new and unrecognizable in the art world, just trying to rise on the ladder. Anything to get out of Harlem. Anything to stop shoveling dirty money for dirty people. Plus, I wasn't a fan of praise and attention. Anything more than a "Hey, that's a cool painting" and I would be stirring nervously and trying to get away from them.

My phone buzzed.

Maxwell had texted me.

Why didn't you just walk over here and tell me what you had to say?

I read the screen and typed back.

Maxwell: We've got a problem.
Me: What?
Maxwell: There's a bunch of shady characters in here.
Me: How shady?
Maxwell: Check the back of the gallery but be careful.

My heart hammered. Anytime Maxwell said be careful, it was a good time to run.

But why would something be dangerous tonight?

This was our night off from our usual activities.

Three years ago, Kennedy, Maxwell, and I had opened this gallery at the young ages of eighteen. Many said we were talented go-getters and a highly motivated youth.

But the ones on the street knew the game. The art gallery was meant for something else. We'd basically opened a laundromat in the hood, but we didn't wash clothes. We cleaned money for a percentage. We dealt with dangerous people, but none of them were too big to fear our life. Low time gangsters.

What's going on now? Can't I get a break from the streets tonight?

I headed in that direction and drank in the people around me. While it was true that many appeared like the typical hipsters, there were some shady characters sprinkled throughout the crowd. Large, muscular men here and there were dressed in black suits and standing by the wall, not looking at the art, just scanning all of the faces. Some had tattoos on their necks. Others had a few scars here or there.

None of the faces were recognizable, but all screamed one thing.

Russians. What the fuck are Russians doing here?

If one looked up the definition for gentrification, they would fine two people-friendly meanings. The first would say that gentrification is the process of improving an area to conform to middle-class taste. The second would say that it was the process of making a person or activity more refined or polite.

Regardless, gentrification had come to my neighborhood. Harlem was a large neighborhood in the northern section of the New York City borough of Manhattan.

These days, there were two types of people that lived in Harlem—the kind that rode the gentrification train over the George Washington bridge and the ones that had lived there all their lives.

I was the latter, but I didn't complain like my friends. Many wanted Harlem to stay the *Black Mecca*. Others embraced the change. I just wanted to sleep without nightmares and not worry about bills. I'd spent long nights in the library reading about the history of Harlem.

This neighborhood had always changed and was destined for continued transformation in the times to come. It had been formed as a Dutch village in the 1600s. After the Civil War, poor Jews and Italians dominated the area. The 1900s brought the Great Migration of blacks, sparking the Harlem Renaissance in the 20's and 30s.

Recently, Harlem's population of blacks had gone down to 40 percent.

And Harlem's crime world was also experiencing a major shift. Gentrification had hit them too. The Russians were moving deeper into Harlem. Many of the Jamaican gangs were getting nervous and talking about war. I just hoped I'd be out of Harlem before things got hot.

But, why are Russians here? What do they want?

A few of these men remained scattered throughout the gallery, but every now and then they glanced to the back of the gallery—right where I was heading.

What's going on?

And then I spotted the center of their attention. A man dressed in a crisp designer suit that was worth so much money, I bet twenties fell from the hems as he walked on by. Unfortunately for me, I didn't see a trail of bills as I followed him.

Who is he?

Slowly, he walked around, drinking in the art.

I matched his speed and lingered five feet away.

He walked by each painting, stopping for a few seconds, and then moving onto the next.

Art enthusiast or here to start trouble?

I continued to keep my distance. When he stopped, I paused and turned in another direction. When he moved on, I inched a little closer.

I had no doubt that all his men knew I was watching him. But, they didn't stop me or say anything. There was no reason to see me as a threat. Where he must've been close to 6'4, I was 5'5.

I know one thing. He's the boss.

He walked like one. Like he owned the ground his feet stepped on. Like he owned the air that we all breathed. Like he could eat up the universe, if he wanted to.

His presence was quite the experience, hitting me with feminine awareness. And speaking of models, he had a perfectly structured face that was ready for fashion, and not the commercial stuff people saw when they stood in line at a grocery. He could've been an editorial model—edgy and high-end. Shoulders a mile wide. Dark hair cut with style. A sleek jaw. His eyebrows were two dark slashes above thick-lashed eyes that glowed blue and deep. Those eyes were moving liquid, but so fucking cold. His lips were tilted at the corners as if he was composing a dirty joke.

He inspired sex. It was an instant shot to my brain and probably to all the other women that watched him walk by. A few licked their lips. Delicious sex. Ungodly primal sex. The dirtiest kind. Up in a filthy alley getting pounded into the brick wall sex. Fucking your boyfriend's best friends sex as he sleeps in the other room. Rough, sheet-clawing sex. Nasty. Grimy sex. And it radiated off every part of him. His face. His presence. His shoulders. His eyes.

My phone buzzed.

I ignored it. It was probably Maxwell telling me to be careful, but this man was intriguing.

I took a chance and got closer, barely two feet away. We both stopped at my focal painting—the one I was most proud of. But I didn't glance at the painting, I drank in the man, as he studied my art with an extreme intensity.

Yeah. Smoking hot. Maybe late twenties or early thirties at the most.

And he continued to study my painting with a fierce indulgence. It was like he was two seconds away from pulling it off the wall and taking it home.

And because of that intensity for my art, it made me want to fuck him. Not that it took much these days. I wished he wasn't this mysterious Russian guy, radiating terror. I wished he was just here for the art. A regular man. If he had been, then I would've fucked him—right on my desk in the office, on my bed at home, and the dirty alley right next to the gallery where I'd taken others for a few minutes and then left them with their pants down, when we were done.

But he wasn't here for art or sex. He'd probably come for something else.

By now, he knew I was next to him. A man like that would've probably known I was following him minutes ago.

Then, let him say something. Let's get this over with.

I edged closer.

This near, the suit looked even more expensive. Where I thought it was hundreds of dollars. I now knew it was thousands. And there was quite an energy under that fabric as he wore it like a second skin. Already, I could make out an impressive muscular frame.

He didn't look my way. Instead he spoke, his voice a deep lovely tone riding a heavy Russian accent, "Why do you paint lions?"

The question shocked me.

He turned my way and centered all his attention on me.

Shocked, I whispered, "I like lions."

"You don't." He put his attention back to the painting. "Your art is captivating. But, it's not until you get to this painting, where I realized you were holding back. This one you love. This one you enjoyed creating and it's not because of the lion."

I turned to the image and tried to see what he saw.

A labyrinth of ropes covered and trapped a lion to the ground. The lion was massive—huge muscles, sharp claws, fangs that protruded out of his mouth. Rage blazed in his eyes. Revenge dripped from his lips, but still, the lion remained trapped to the ground. I'd made the creature in tiny crystals and used oil paint for certain details and outlining of him. I'd used threads from actual rope to painstakingly place a confusing labyrinth on him. It couldn't just be a trap. It had to be more. The lion looked exhausted. One could tell that he'd struggled for a long time, trying to get out.

Lucky for him, a little mouse sat in the corner, nibbling away at the rope, ready to free him. It had taken me weeks to work on that little mouse. In some ways it was 3D, pushing out from the canvas—mink fur, ruby eyes, a tail of gray roped crystals that trailed beyond the image.

"You don't like lions," he said. "But, you do like mice. That's the best mouse I've ever seen."

"I do like rats and mice," I admitted. "They're crafty and hard to kill."

He looked at me. "And so smart they can even help lions."

"Yes."

"You're a talented artist."

I felt weird about the compliment, but I forced a smile. "Thank you."

"Nice to meet you, Emily." He extended his hand, and I slid my fingers into his warm grip. "My name is Kazimir."

Maybe you can mention why you already know my name.

I couldn't breathe. I tried to pull away my hand, but he kept his fingers firmly around mine as he studied me. After a few seconds, he let go.

I recovered. "Are you a big fan of art?"

"My mother named me after the famous artist Kazimir Malevich. Have you ever heard of him?"

"Yes, but only a little. He was one of the originators of the avant-garde movement, pushing for nontraditional art and creative innovation. He liked to break the rules."

"Yes, he did." Kazimir smiled at me. "Did you go to art school?"

"No." I looked away. "You could say that I was homeschooled."

"Hmmm. There's a story behind what you said."

"A small one."

"Tell me, unless it's a secret."

"I don't like secrets and besides I've talked about this to a few journalists." I sighed. "My brothers and I had some rough times during our childhood."

He nodded. "I definitely know about rough childhoods."

I gave him a half smile. "We...lost our home and our parents, when we were young. Neither of us were a fan of foster care so we would run away and meet up at the library. It was the best place to sleep during the winter. All we had to do was hide around closing. Once all the staff left, we would spend the night reading to each other."

"You said brothers. You have more than one?"

"I have one that is my blood and one that's basically a *brother from another mother.*"

He raised his eyebrows.

"Basically, we're so close we're family."

"I like your story. You're a survivor."

"Most are. Who really has it easy in this world?"

He gestured to the lion and mouse. "This painting is like our situation."

My voice lowered. "*Our* situation?"

He inched closer to me and smiled. "Like the lion in this painting, trapped by rope and other things, I need your help. I need you to be a little mouse and nibble away the problem. And when you do this for me, you'll find there will be many rewards."

I knew killers and powerful men, and he wasn't just one of them, he was *the one*. I doubted many men were above him.

Granted, he had the model perfect chiseled angles and beautifully masculine face, but those eyes screamed death. Most had normal windows to the soul. Kids had innocence and adventure pooled along their pupils. Older people had this weariness in theirs. But his eyes. There was no warmth. They were cold and lacking humanity.

He smiled. "Do you think you can help?"

I doubt it, but I'm totally down to help you not kill me.

I swallowed. "How can I help you?"

He studied me so intently, I felt stripped bare. "Let's go to your office and discuss it."

"Okay. Let me just let my partners know." *Maxwell, get the guns just in case. Kennedy, call my brother.* "They'll have to take up the slack for hosting my event."

He nodded and followed me as I walked off.

Maxwell was already heading my way. Him and I met in the center of the gallery.

Watching Kazimir the whole time, Maxwell stepped to my side and whispered. "What's up?"

I whispered back, "I don't know. He wants to talk. He's Russian."

"Obviously."

"His first name is Kazimir. Look him up and ask around. It also wouldn't hurt to get a gun or two."

"Okay." Maxwell eyed Kazimir behind me. "Where are you two going?"

"My office."

Maxwell frowned.

"I'll be fine. If he wanted me dead, I would be dead. This probably deals with the Jamaicans."

Maxwell shook his head. "Or it deals with your brother."

My calm shifted to nervousness. It was one thing to have the Russian mob at my art showing. It was another thing to have them there due to Darryl. Anytime people came knocking because of him, I had to do bad things.

"Let's hope this doesn't deal with Darryl." I looked around. "Where's Kennedy?"

"As soon as she spotted the Russians, she left."

"Left?"

"Left."

What the fuck?

"Okay. That's fine." I sighed. "I'll be back. This is probably no big deal."

Maxwell didn't look convinced. "Be careful. I'll check him out."

I left Maxwell and guided Kazimir to my office. With each step, his men moved from their positions in the gallery and followed us.

Most of the regular art enthusiasts paused from their conversations and looked to see what was going on. Anybody who didn't know much about the crime world would've probably thought he was some high political figure and his men were secret service.

But a few knew what was up. They spotted Kazimir and his men and headed to the exit.

I had no doubt that by tomorrow morning, everyone in Harlem would know the Russian mob had come to my gallery. I just hoped none of this would get me in trouble. Working for criminals meant walking a tight rope each day. The trick was doing exactly what they said without the tiniest error because one problem could mean the end of my life or those around me.

It wasn't the easiest job, but it kept me closer to getting the hell out of New York.

He'd said that he was like the lion in the picture and I would be his mouse nibbling away.

I don't know about that. I just hope this lion doesn't eat the mouse.

Chapter 3
Kazimir

She was beautiful and very dangerous. The beauty was easy to spot on her, but the danger. . .it crept behind her eyes. She was scared, but not terrified. She was compliant and open to what I had to say, but not shaking in her heels.

I'll have to watch this one.

I hadn't survived and prospered in the Bratva on killing alone. Intelligence, lethal skills, and physical ability were awesome qualities to fill my résumé, but my advantage came from my natural instincts. And those instincts were telling me that Emily was more than what met my eyes. Much more dangerous than she appeared. Not many women incited this.

She showed me to her office and I looked her up and down, admiring that lovely body. She had on a tight white skirt with a cream-colored top. Against those breasts, the top was too small to be legal. Her tiny waist exaggerated those curvy hips and ass.

She dressed in all white, but she's no angel. What's her story?

She unlocked her door. I stepped inside and gestured for my men to stay behind. My brother Sasha remained outside with the paintings.

The door closed behind me.

She went to the other side of the desk and sat down. I immediately hated the distance between us, thinking I would've gotten to touch her hand again. When she sat down, our gazes met.

Her eyes were big and bright as the full moon, casting a magical glow across her face. This close and without any distractions from the people in the gallery or even my men, I realized those eyes weren't simply brown. Tiny flecks of green and gold illuminated the irises.

For a moment, I found myself lost in those liquid depths, wondering what secrets lay hidden beneath.

Her sexy voice sliced through the quiet. "How can I help you?"

"If one needed millions washed, how would they do it?"

She raised her eyebrows as if shocked that I went right into it. But I had no time for fun banter. I had money that needed to be clean.

She folded her hands and placed them on the desk. "I've never cleaned anything over half a million."

"Then, congratulations." I smiled. "You've been promoted."

She frowned but said nothing.

"How would you clean millions?" I asked. "This is hypothetical of course."

I'd been ahead of the FBI for years, having my own men planted in many of the departments, but I still didn't like talking at locations that had not been checked by my people. My wording would have to be careful, yet still deliver the required message.

"Millions?" She blew out a long breath.

"Be quick, Mrs. Chambers. Your brother's life depends on it. Again, this is all hypothetical."

Her face shifted to worry. "My brother is involved?"

"Is that your final answer?"

"No." She cleared her throat. "How would I wash millions? I would find someone who was already rich or at least coming up on a big inheritance, they would be easier to control and funnel money through. That person could get the capitol from a bank to borrow massive loans, ones that wouldn't make the government suspicious, when his bank account begins to fill. I'd have the person buy huge, expensive properties which is easy to do in New York. Everything is overpriced. Purchasing buildings are good for washing huge amounts. For millions, we're talking skyscrapers. There would be fake office spaces, fake tenants, trumped up construction bills, etc."

"Interesting." I watched her. "Then, I'll talk to you tomorrow."

"Tomorrow? Where?"

"I'll pick you up from your place. Haven Street, right?"

Fear hit her eyes, when I said her address, but she kept her voice calm. "Yes. I live on Haven Street."

"I'll see you again at eight in the morning."

"Okay." She rose when I did. "And...my brother?"

"He's gotten himself into some trouble, but you can help. You're very smart. There should be no problems."

She gripped the edge of her desk. For a second, I didn't like that reaction, I didn't want her that scared of me. But that was only for a second and then she walked around her desk.

"So...my brother is safe?"

"He is."

He probably won't be able to move his right shoulder anymore, but he can move everything else for now.

"When will I get to see him?" she asked.

"When you've showed me that I can trust you. For now, he stays with me. But don't worry. He's got a bed and my people will keep him safe. There's no need for people to die from neglect. In fact, you should see this as a big opportunity for a new career. I've only known your name for an hour and had my men ask around. Many claim you've helped a lot of unsavory characters. Apparently, you're the queen of...how do they say it...frenemies."

"Bad guys aren't always bad people."

"Then, we'll have a happy partnership."

She stirred but forced herself to smile. "I agree. I'm willing to do anything to keep my brother safe. Let me know, and I can figure it out. You'll be happy."

My mind drifted to the other ways she could make me happy and then I pulled my imagination back. If someone killed my washer, then they were trying to stop my money in New York. Everyone knew, if you owned New York, you owned America. And I enjoyed my hold on this country. But, someone thought they could do a better job. It was time to focus on the war ahead. I figured it would be small and take no more than a week.

What could this country do to me, that my own country hadn't already done?

I'd been born into death, so I welcomed it, whenever it rang.

I walked off, paused, and then turned around. "You never told me why you painted the lions."

"Someone commissioned me to do it."

Coincidence or connected?

"Who?" I asked.

"I don't know. It was an anonymous person which isn't really a huge deal in the art world. I was asked to paint them three months ago, do a showing, and then deliver on a particular date. Which happens to be tomorrow."

"But, you don't know who commissioned you?"

"No."

I mentally filed it away. In life, things happened for a reason. Instinct told me to pay attention to everything, even the little things. Nothing ever was a true coincidence. One could always find a connection in the tiniest moments.

"When you find out who commissioned the paintings, let me know."

She scrunched her face in confusion, but then shifted it back to neutral. "I will."

"And the painting with the lion and the mouse, I'm buying that one. You'll have to explain that to your buyer. If he doesn't like it, then I'll explain it."

She widened her eyes and nodded.

"How much?" I asked.

"I hadn't thought of a price for any of them, since the person had already paid."

"Then, I'll come up with my own price and have my men pick it up after the showing."

"Sounds good." She walked over to the door and opened it.

I left and found the whole situation more pleasing than any other business dealing I could think of. While she must've been scared, she handled it well. I'd had men urinate right in front of me, so scared they couldn't control their bladder. I had women try to run, before I'd even presented my question. Other women came on to me sexually to get their way. And then there were the ones who tried to babble out of working with me, begging for their lives, pleading for their freedom.

This wasn't her. She was compliant and straightforward. It felt more like a business interview than anything else.

There's something more to her.

When the office door closed, I gestured for one of my men. "Put ears and eyes on her."

"Yes, sir. They've already installed cameras inside her brownstone, but they haven't finished yet."

"Good." I headed out of the hallway and met with Sasha who stared at a family of lions tearing an antelope apart. Instead of red paint, the blood sparkled with crimson gems.

"I love her work," Sasha said.

"She's talented and beautiful. This will be fun."

Sasha eyed me. "How much fun are you planning to have, brother?"

"Do you see the subject of her paintings?"

"Yes." He rolled his eyes. "The lions."

"It means something."

We walked off.

"Fine." Sasha waved me away. "It means something. Perhaps, it means good luck."

I glanced back at the painting I'd bought. "But, the lion is caught in the net."

"And the mouse helps get him out."

We stepped outside. The night air chilled my skin.

"Then, she will be my mouse." I headed to the limo.

"No, she will be *our washer*. I hate when you do your sync thing. It always gets us into trouble."

"It's synchronicity and I've showed you hundreds of times that it works. We wouldn't be here, if not for *meaningful coincidences*. Carl Jung believed that—"

"Carl Jung is dead, and you will be to, if you don't stop with your meaningful coincidences."

"There's no such thing as a coincidence, my friend. It's all connected." I tapped the side of my head. "That's what keeps us ahead of everyone else. I keep my eyes open."

"You keep your eyes open? That's why?" Sasha laughed. "Maybe, we're also ahead of everyone else, because you don't mind peeling the skin off men one strip at a time, when they betray you."

"Loyalty keeps us strong."

"I agree, so leave your dead man and his meaningful coincidences alone, as well as this mouse."

I smiled. "*Mysh*. That's what I will call her. My little mouse."

Sasha laughed again. "I think you're just looking for an excuse to fuck her."

"I don't need to create one. She's beautiful and smart. That's enough."

"Well, she's not for fucking, but if she doesn't clean this money, maybe you can fuck her right before I kill her."

I ignored him. Killing women was his thing, not mine. When he saw a beautiful lady, he thought of the ways he could make her scream. Whereas I just wanted to make her moan.

"Do you think she can handle this?" Sasha asked.

"The universe will decide. So far, the lion is trapped in rope and the mouse is getting him out. Is it a meaningful coincidence or is it my destiny?"

"Destinies and meaningful coincidences." Sasha pointed to a billboard. "Look there. That's a lion with his cock cut off. There's your sign. What does that say?"

I looked at the billboard. It was empty. "You just make sure someone is watching her."

"Of course. For now, she's the most important person in this shitty country. I sent Ivan in."

"Have Ivan send the footage of her place to my phone."

"I did." He frowned. "I never forget how much you enjoy watching people. Where do we go next?"

"The night is still early. I want to meet Penelope and find out more about this missing hooker."

Sasha's frown deepened. "Hookers and brothels. Will the fun ever end?"

"We're in New York. This city never sleeps."

"And if we go to a brothel tonight, we won't sleep either."

"Then, we should eat first. The Russian Tea Room?" I asked. "You always talk about it."

"Of course. You will like it. Good traditional cuisine, yet in luxury as you like it."

"We only live once."

"This is true."

The limo drove off, and I gazed at the beauty of this city. Skyscrapers glittered within the stars and moonlight. The streets hummed with cars honking and people cursing or chattering in their phones as they rushed off to this place or that that. Oily smoke from taxis' rusted-exhausts mingled with the street foot vendors roasted scents.

When I was a kid, I never thought I would be in a magical place like this.

DIRTY KISSES

Life had been strange for me.

I was born in 1991, months before the Soviet Union's hammer and sickle flag lowered for the last time over the Kremlin, later replaced by the Russian tricolor on December 25th. Months before, Mikhail Gorbachev resigned as president of the Soviet Union, leaving Boris Yeltsin to lead the newly independent Russian state.

During the Soviet Union's communist rule, they deported entire criminal communities of various ethnicities out of their homelands. Many were my ancestors who were forced to live n the Southwest of the U.S.S.R.

They thought it was a solution to crime, but the area quickly developed into powerful ghettos corroded with criminals. And among the poorest were my father's clan—Siberians. Rough and Raw and damn near unstoppable.

I was born there.

Even after Russia was formed, and my father later died, leaving my mother to fend for herself, I remained there—hungry, deadly, and ready to rip the world alive. My uncles taught me that we were the honest criminals. The rest were power-hungry political and murderous bureaucrats that had their minions—cops and other devils in uniforms—do their work.

My education didn't come from schools. It came from the streets, and nothing as pretty as found in New York. My home ran with snow-covered muddy roads flanked by shacks. Many times, blood stained the snow, and most of the time the corpse wore a uniform.

At eight, I learned how to stab a person properly from my mother. She'd hung dead animals from the ceiling and I stabbed them, learning the right organs to puncture first. Hearing the sound, the right cut would make against flesh.

At ten, I'd already had a little gang—my young sister Valentina and five cousins. They gave me my few happy memories of winter. We would stand around a trash can full of fire and sip vodka we'd stolen from our uncles. There, we boasted about all the money we would one day have.

By our teens, we stole from the rich and gave to the poor. Anything taken or gained—no matter how big or small—was brought back to the neighborhood—generations of outcasted criminals living together. Any food and money went to the mothers. Weapons and drugs went to the men.

Anybody on the outside was the enemy, and I hated them. And from that disgust, a rage of violence lived in my eyes.

Sasha's father came to our area, when I turned fifteen. He fell in love with my mother. Still married, he moved us to Moscow. His wife died under mysterious reasons and my mother took her place.

And that was where the beast inside of me really grew.

On the day my mother died, diamonds covered her neck and fingers. Furs wrapped around her body.

She smiled at me. "Kazimir, you must control the rage."

"I have, mother."

"No." She coughed. "I can still see it in your eyes."

"Then, stay so you can help take it away."

Her face grew sad. "I can't, Kazimir, but one day someone will."

The limo continued through Manhattan and I thought back to Emily's eyes. I couldn't see through them. They were locked doors inside of her pupils, hiding big secrets within.

What secrets do you have behind them, Emily? And why do I so badly want to know them?

Chapter 4
Maxwell

Fuck. The Russians are already here. I thought I had more time.

Benjamin Franklin said, "Three may keep a secret, if two of them are dead."

I should've taken Franklin's advice last night. Maybe the Russians wouldn't have showed up at Emily's art showing. Maybe all of the Tinder Killer stuff would've gone away.

Darryl, you stupid bastard. How could you send them her way? And where the fuck is Kennedy?

We'd all grown up together in the same shitty building—Darryl, Emily, Kennedy, and me. After the fire, everything changed. We all moved. Years later, Emily bought the burnt up building, getting it repaired with dirty money, and renovating our old apartments. Emily didn't show how broken she was, but when she bought the property, we knew she still struggled with the pain. And me being the physical embodiment of her guilt and battered conscience, I felt bad and moved in with her, hating every brick in place, every wall, every step, every door.

Emily and I still resided there—she stayed in her parents' old apartment and I lived in my father's old place.

The other two thought we were crazy. Kennedy never came to visit. Darryl came, but didn't stay for too long—always jittery and stirring, never sitting down. Sometimes he swore he heard ghosts whispering and would just leave.

I didn't mind the ghosts. Neither did Emily.

But the secrets... those were the motherfuckers that I despised. Secrets killed people. They broke up homes and destroyed families. They simmered in murky evil and waited until everything was going great in life to rise up and poison.

Tonight, I was holding onto a secret that could get us all killed, and I had no idea how to save us.

And what about the girl? There's too much in my head!

But I was getting too ahead of myself. I had to think of everything that had happened before these Russians showed up at Emily's event.

I walked outside and breathed for a few minutes, running the past twenty-four hours in my head.

Why the hell did I answer that phone call?

Last night, as usual, I'd been cleaning up everyone's mess. I got the phone call, grabbed my bag of tools, ran to Rumi's place, and walked into some fucked up shit.

I should've never answered the damn phone.

Rumi lay on the floor with a knifed-out smile. I'd put on my gloves, cut open his stomach, and yanked out his intestines. Pink and slimy, they slithered out. A rank smell filled the air.

"What the fuck are you doing?" Darryl paced on my side.

"I'm making it look like a Russian hit." I pulled the intestines out more and wrapped the bloody thick rope around his neck.

"Is that how they do it?"

"I don't fucking know."

Darryl held his stomach. "You're fucking sick. That's a dead body, man."

"I'm not the sick one." I smeared blood on Rumi's chest and tried to breathe through the funk. "If I'm so sick, then you should've called someone else."

"Oh fuck, I'm going to throw up."

"Get out of here. I don't need more shit to clean up. Why don't you handle Emily?"

"Fine."

"And don't call anyone."

"I won't." He rushed away.

Motherfucker.

I should've never answered the fucking call.

Why did I do it?

At Rumi's place, I finished my work. Minutes later the door opened. I figured it was Darryl, but then a muffled cry snapped my eyes away from Rumi's corpse.

A black woman stood behind me, shaking. She was young, probably eighteen or nineteen. She'd dressed for seduction—matching red panties and a tiny bra that did nothing to hold her huge breasts. So scared, her scream had been lost in her throat. She just stood there with her mouth open and her hands caught in mid-air.

Fuck.

She ran off.

"No! Don't go!" *I grabbed my gun and took off after her, racing down the hall. She shoved shelves of dildos as if to block my way. Huge plastic penises rained down and coated the floor. I almost tripped a few times.*

Sick fuck. How many dicks did you need, Rumi?

I jumped over some more as she slammed the hallway door closed. Her footsteps sounded far off.

"Wait!" *I rushed to open it and caught her image down by the front door.* "Hold up! I won't hurt you."

She screamed. Her ass jiggled in those tiny panties. It wasn't the best time for a reaction, but my dick jerked to attention.

I might've caught her faster, if I hadn't been a little bit distracted by her body.

She got to the front door and fumbled with the lock. Fear had her focus fucked up. She checked over her shoulder. Tears ran down her face. Dread hit her eyes.

"Hey, I won't hurt you." *I sped up and caged her body to the door, taking her into my arms and covering her mouth.* "Listen. I know what it looks like, but it isn't it."

She trembled against me, barely reaching the center of my chest. There was no ring on her finger, no husband waiting for her to get home, but there could've been a boyfriend. Not that I should've cared.

Her long dark hair hung in loose braids over one shoulder. Her skin was soft and creamy, and I had an urge to know what it felt like. I leaned in a little, getting the smell of strawberries and honey. I didn't know someone could smell sweet like that, and my mouth watered.

"I won't hurt you." *I released one of my hands from the door and run my finger down her cheek. I needed to find out just how soft her skin really was. The desire to touch her overwhelmed.*

She glanced over her shoulder.

Our gazes met.

"Please don't hurt me," *she whispered, pulling me from the trance she had me under.*

"I won't hurt you, but I can't just let you go either."

She whimpered.

Motherfucker. What am I going to do with her?

It would've been easier to kill her, but that wasn't me. I never played that roll. I cleaned up shit. I buried secrets. I hid things. I crept in shadows, watching shit go down.

"I'll let go of you, if you don't scream."

She nodded.

I let go and showed her my gun.

She shrieked and then covered her own mouth.

"You and I are the same. Okay?"

She whimpered but bobbed her head.

"We're the same because we both walked into some fucked up shit and now we have to figure out a way to get out of this without no one killing us." *I had to keep on talking. Her body distracted me. So close and pressed against her, my dick came alive, wanting to touch her more. But, this wasn't the time or place, and I needed to get her out of here, before someone tried to kill her.*

"Please." She struggled against my hold, rubbing that soft ass against my dick. *"I'll do anything. Just let me go."*

Anything? No. Stop. I've got shit to do.

I gritted my teeth, wondering why she was even here, half-naked and so sexy. Rumi liked hookers—young ones—and she looked innocent as hell.

"How old are you?" I asked.

"Nineteen."

"Jesus." I turned her around and forced my dick to calm down.

She gazed up at me with those sweet eyes. "I-I won't t-tell anyone."

"I know." I sighed. "But, just in case. . .I have to make sure."

"Please, don't hurt me."

"I'm sorry." I leaned away and tightened the grip on my gun. "Remember. I'm sorry."

"Wha—"

I slammed her head with the butt of the gun. She fell to the floor, blinking her eyes and then closing them.

Kennedy would've killed me, if she saw it. Emily would've beaten my ass herself. And my mother, would've helped them both tear my behind up.

Sorry, ladies, but knocking her out is better than murdering her.

I let go of last night's memories and blew out a long breath.

This week was the wrong time to quit cigarettes. My fingers itched to light something. My lungs yearned to burn.

My mind returned to the present moment. Back to Emily's art showing. Back to the current problem.

Why did the Russian want to talk to Emily?

I stood outside the gallery, trying to keep myself calm. Things were too close to getting out of hand.

The front door opened.

The Russians walked out. Two rich scary looking men flanked by ten others. The two rich ones got in the limo, talking to each other the whole time. Neither saw me.

I glanced over my shoulder and looked through the gallery's glass wall. Emily had returned to her event, slowly walking around. Whatever she'd talked about with the Russians didn't show on her face.

I have to find out what they said to her. Why the fuck would Darryl tell them to come here? It doesn't make any sense. And where the fuck is Kennedy?!

I pulled out my phone and texted her.

Me: Where are you?

Kennedy: Home.

Me: Why?

Kennedy: I'm sick. I need some rest.

She'd seemed just fine an hour ago. In fact, it wasn't until I pointed out the Russians to her that she disappeared.

There's some other shit going on that I don't know about.

I texted Darryl.

Me: Where are you? We need to talk.

No response came.

Maybe the Russians had them. At this point, I didn't know if that was a good thing or not. Cleaning up after his sister and him was getting to be exhausting. I almost wished the Russians would keep his ass for the rest of the year.

And what about the girl? Maybe, she woke up.

I'd wrapped her up in one of Rumi's massive suitcases and rolled it out. She was now in my guest bedroom, tied and lying on the bed. Her mouth duct taped. My soul crumbled from having to do it.

What the fuck am I going to do with her?

At Rumi's place, I'd wiped down as many fingerprints as I could think of. I doubted they'd even find Rumi's own prints in that house. I took the security footage, knife, and everything else. I should've been a little bit more relieved, but instead a tornado of worry tore through my gut. By the time I got the girl and I back to the house, it was morning. I tied her hands and legs, taped her mouth, and then placed her on my bed.

How could I be so stupid? I thought this was the end, but I think this is just the beginning. Maybe, I can get her a plane ticket out of her or something.

I would just have to wait until this Russian shit settled over.

My phone buzzed.

I checked the text, hoping it was Darryl.

Emily: Meet me at your place in an hour.

I thought of the half-naked woman trapped in my bed. The last thing Emily needed to know was that I'd kidnapped someone.

Me: My place isn't good for tonight. Let's meet at yours.

Emily: I might have a pest control problem. Let's meet at yours.

Pest control? Bugs. Fuck. She thinks they're going to bug her.

Technology elevated everyone's game. I handled a lot of freelance jobs for lowlifes who wanted to monitor their workers or enemies. I had a special love for the mini cameras. People could put things anywhere and monitor a person's every movement. But the smart gangs used this too and it appeared the Russians were on point.

Me: Then, we meet at X's. My place is a no for tonight.

I knew she wouldn't want to get Xavier involved. She always felt guilty with him. But, more people needed to be involved. Whether she understood it or not, the bodies were already piling up. And goddamn it, I needed help keeping secrets.

Emily: Let's not get X in this. Why not your place? I don't care, if it's a mess. We're not having high tea, Max! We need to talk.

Me: Doesn't matter. Not my place. I'll see you at X's in an hour.

I shut the phone off and headed to Darryl's, hoping I could swing by to see Kennedy too. She said she was sick. I thought it was bullshit. Kennedy knew something, more than I did. Darryl was hiding something, and Emily was a goddamn nuclear weapon with a shattered mind.

Fuck that. I can't deal with all this by myself.

Chapter 5
Emily

Kazimir left my office.

He mentioned he represented the lion in that painting and I was the mouse. I didn't doubt it. He damn sure looked like a lion to me—a ferocious one ready to eat me alive. I'd dealt with dangerous people, but this was out of my league.

Every second, minute, hour, and day had to run perfectly. There could be no slip ups, and there wasn't many to trust. Not even Darryl, he'd just end up getting me into more bullshit.

The art showing went on, but I was barely there mentally.

In my office, I changed out of my Cynthia personality, leaving the wig, heels, and outfit there. My afro was braided into a valley of small cornrows formed into tiny designs—spirals and swirls going around my head and then down. The many ends dangled well past my shoulders and curled at the tip. I had a girl in the projects that could braid hair anyway. She could braid a person's name on the right side of the head and put a bunch of hearts on the left.

I put on jeans, sneakers, and a black jacket. I pulled out my desk drawer and stared at my gun.

Should I bring it with me?

I sighed and shut the drawer. The chances of my using it would be low. If these Russians wanted me dead for some reason, they would be better at pulling out their guns and shooting than me. I thought of what Uncle Xavier had told me years ago.

"You're not a shooter. Put the gun down. Besides, you're the most dangerous weapon on the block—a woman with a brain that can outthink anybody."

I shut the drawer.

I shifted into my new persona. The only thing I kept on me was my heart locket—the one my Uncle had given me for Christmas last year. While he wasn't really my Uncle, he'd been there for me more than anyone had.

"Keep this with you, Em." He placed it around my neck. *"I want to always be with you."*

I headed off to meet Maxwell at Xavier's. After I closed the event, I spied two cars across the street. I checked the back of the building and two Russians stood outside, talking to each other and smoking cigarettes.

He already has them watching me. That makes sense.

Too bad, I didn't like being watched. I shut off all the lights in the gallery, opened the utility closet, lifted the hatch on the floor, grabbed my trusty flashlight, and climbed down into the abandoned tunnel under my property. It was the main reason why I'd bought it.

Working with criminals wasn't an easy feat. Some came to me drugged up on power, ego, or whatever they'd sniffed, smoked, or injected. Sometimes, it was better to have several escape routes mapped out for a safe departure.

This lion is keeping me in the dark for now. He doesn't need to know my movements or where I am tonight.

I slammed the latch closed and traveled in the directions of Xavier's lair.

When people thought of the New York City underground, the vast subway system, sewers, and water tunnels came to mind. Far lesser people knew of the obscure and lesser documented tunnels—often running from building to building and throughout Manhattan. When we were kids, Maxwell, Darryl, and I had found the first hidden tunnel by accident. That night, I'd checked the records on it at the library, overly obsessed with the idea of secret tunnels and hidden passageways that many didn't know about.

DIRTY KISSES

It was the Farley-Morgan tunnel right under 9th avenue. The records had reported that it was an old postal tunnel that ran under the east side of 9th avenue between the Morgan mail sorting facility and the basement of the famous James A. Farley post office. The heavily secured road tunnel was used to move mail to and from Penn Station, where letters and packages would be transported on Amtrak trains. Apparently, Amtrak even had a special mail only train for a few years, running along the northeast corridor. They stopped using the passageway in the 2000s. That tunnel became our playground—our haven from the gangs trying to recruit us, the social workers searching for us, and the creepy guys taking too much of an interest in little kids alone on the streets.

Regardless, I became obsessed with finding secret tunnels throughout New York, spending weeks reading through books in the library and then dragging Maxwell and Darryl to search them out. There were the McCarren Pool tunnels in Brooklyn. McCarren was the borough's biggest public pool. The tunnels had been built for behind-the-scenes passages for maintenance employees, boiler room access, etc. It was a huge network leading all over the place. We must've ran through those for weeks.

People wouldn't believe how many passageways had been built and hidden right under them. There was the East New York freight tunnel more widely known among graffiti artists. Columbia University had an old steam tunnel system that dated back to when the campus was an insane asylum. There were even ones under Rockefeller center.

However, Harlem had a labyrinth of tunnels not on record. I couldn't find one ounce of information in the library and later online of why they existed. The most I could think of was that the tunnels must've been made back in the 1800s and the records were lost.

With the latch shut, only a black quiet surrounded me.

I shut on the flashlight and finished my journey down the ladder.

Under the city, there was only silence, darkness, and rats. They scurried along, so unused to humans they steered clear of me when I walked forward. At times, I made my walk through here, instead of dealing with the hustle and bustle of the streets. Kennedy came down once and went right back up, scared out of her mind of being down here.

But for some reason, this labyrinth had been my home. And at the scariest times of my life, I sought the tunnel's hidden comfort over anything else.

Down here I contemplated the craziness that had just happened.

As usual, Darryl had brought trouble to my door.

"Like the lion in this painting, trapped by rope and other things, I need your help. I need you to be a little mouse and nibble away the problem," He'd said. *"And when you do this for me, you'll find there will be many rewards."*

Kazimir had asked a question about money laundering. Clearly, he wanted me to clean his dirty money.

Why me? There's tons of more capable people in New York, probably hungry and willing to do anything for him.

My plan had been to get out of this shady business. I hoped my art would be the train riding me away.

Fucking Darryl. How the hell did you get in trouble with them?

That was the biggest problem. I could wash the lion's money. I could do any damn thing he needed, as long as my brother was safe.

But is he safe? And what did he do to get in the lion's claws to begin with?

That was the biggest problem. The money was a task. The labyrinth of trouble my brother always had me navigating through was what would give me gray hairs before I reached my sixties.

Maybe that was why I loved moving through these dark tunnels. It was like life. I constantly navigatedf a network of darkness, structured like a spider's web. It was easy to get lost and much easier to be bitten by spiders. One had to move through the deceitful corners and search out the passageways with no map at all, just instinct and the need to survive.

Fucking Darryl. If the Russians don't kill him, I will.

Footsteps echoed through the tunnel. My flashlight served as my only guidance, creating a glowing path in front of me.

Kazimir's sexy face appeared in my head. I didn't want to admit it, but I couldn't believe how handsome he was. His midnight-black hair looked like he'd been running his fingers through it. His slacks molded to his legs perfectly. Upon seeing him, I wanted to sleep with him. Had he been at my art showing for anything else, I would've fucked him.

Ignore the sexiness and focus.

I decided in that moment to never think of him as Kazimir. The name was just as hot and unique as the man, and I didn't need to be thinking of sexy. I had to stay focused.

It took me less than twenty minutes to get to the pink ribboned ladder, signaling for my block. I'd tied the ribbons on years ago. Now they appeared frazzled and moth eaten. I shut the flashlight off and climbed up.

The cool night air hit my skin as I clambered out of the sewer and into an alley between 153rd and 155th street—three blocks down from my home.

After the silence of the tunnels, the city's noise scratched against my senses. It took me time to adjust as I slammed the sewer top down and left the alley. Music and chatter blasted from the yellow painted Bodega across the street. I went in there all the time. The owner, Paco kept an old radio on the ice machine. On a Friday night like tonight, he loved to pop some cassette tapes in and talk crap and drink with the guys crowded in front.

A dirty, wrinkled newspaper rolled along the sidewalk. On the cover there was a huge question mark dripping in blood. The headline read, "Who's the Tinder Killer?"

The wind blew at the newspaper, turning the page.

A black man displayed on the next page talking about another story. I recognized the dead man's face from the news. Two men and he had been shot over fifty times by plainclothes police. It had sparked from some out of hand bar fight in Queens and then spun out of control. The worst part was that he died the day before his wedding. Everybody had been angry about it, causing long debates in laundromats and almost fist fights out in the streets.

I passed the paper and moved on.

Further down the side streets, old brownstones that had been purchased and renovated. FOR SALE signs sat in their front yards.

It took me ten more minutes to get to Xavier's.

It was a lair. That was the only way to describe it. He didn't live inside a house or building. Instead he'd used an old abandoned school bus—one of those small ones to transport disabled children. Holes decorated the sides. He'd taken on the tires, dragged it back into an alley on the side of our old building, and blacked out the windows. In the back of the vehicle, he's made a bed of the seats. In the front, his guests could lounge on painted crates and check out his little makeshift shelves full of technical equipment. There were tiny hidden cameras planted on the top of the bus's roof and in the headlights. He used a battery-operated hot plate for food. During the winter, he had a battery-operated heater. Usually, he hung out in the bus driver's seat a lot, reading and checking his security footage every now and then. There was an outhouse that he'd hid further down in the alley. God only knew how and where he emptied. I damn sure never asked.

Xavier had been my neighbor long ago. I didn't like to think about those times, when we all lived in that building. None of us liked the past. And even when I purchased the building, Xavier was the main person against it, refusing to move into the vacant apartments I'd had renovated for him.

"I'll never go back there." Xavier pointed at me. "Don't you ever bring that place up to me again."

And I never did. We pretended like the building never existed, that our past never happened. And I visited and brought him things when I could. Unfortunately, I had nothing to give this night. Instead, I'd come for advice and answers.

I entered the alley. The bus's door was open. Maxwell stood next to the outside of the bus.

Xavier sat on the bus's steps, scratching his salt and pepper beard. He'd gone bald and shaved the rough afro he usually wore. Due to the smooth cut, the tattoos on his head were exposed. All-star constellations inked on his dark brown skin.

Xavier ran his fingers through that beard again and sneered. "You two can't stay out of trouble."

"I see Max has caught you up." I gave Xavier a hug, closing my nose to the funk and grime that covered him like a second skin. I let him go and stepped back. "What do you think about our situation?"

Xavier lit a joint and inhaled. "I knew something was odd, when I saw a bunch of tech vehicles parked down by *that place*."

That place was the building where I lived.

"Men were sneaking in that motherfucker like people aren't going to notice." Xavier offered the joint to Max.

Max shook his head and then looked at me. "The crime world doesn't inspire trust. So, we're sure they have cameras and bugs all in there. Be careful what you say and do, Emily, but don't act like you know they're watching."

I shrugged. "This isn't the first time someone's tried this. We'll be fine. I'm more worried about why they want me to wash money for them."

Max let out a long breath. "That's what the fuck they want? Why *you* of all people? I mean you're efficient, but—"

"It doesn't matter why," Xavier said. "All that matters is you need to do that shit, and do it perfectly. No half steps. No fuck ups or your ass is dead."

"Great pep talk." I crossed my arms over my chest. "Have you heard anything around Harlem, X?"

"The biggest news is Rumi is dead." Xavier blew out smoke. "TV and cops say it was a suicide. Everyone on the streets say he was killed. And it's all types of stories. Some say the Jamaicans did it. Rumi never got along with them. Others say Rumi liked some nasty shit, when it came to sex, and it went too far. Motherfucker died orgasming."

Maxwell shook his head. "Harlem has always had some of the best storytellers."

My heart stopped for a few seconds. I had this awful anxiety in my gut. All of this was directly related and now everything was making sense.

"Who do you think did it?" I asked.

Maxwell shrugged. "It doesn't matter. That's not our problem."

"Suicide or not, Rumi washed for the Russians." I began piecing everything together. "He dies. They're looking for who did it, but most importantly they need their money cleaned. They go to Darryl because his name is all over the records."

"I told you not to do that." Xavier coughed into his hand.

"If I didn't have Darryl connected to the businesses, Rumi would've bothered him or worse."

And then Xavier went into what we liked to call his preacher mode. "Darryl didn't have to fucking work for Rumi in the first place, and you damn sure didn't have to clean up his messes. You should have stayed out of the whole situation with Darryl and Rumi years ago, but you can't because you like to be the big sister to the rescue. And now, look at where you are? You thought you've created a solution back in the days, and what you did was build a trap around you."

"Thanks for the positivity, X, but I need answers, not advice that I won't listen to anyway."

"Stubborn." He took another puff of his joint.

"If he put cameras in there, I can't turn them off, but I at least want to know where they are."

Smoke left Xavier's lips. "The easiest way to detect hidden cameras is checking around the place carefully. An inch-by-inch search to find the obvious ones. Those men were in and out your place in less than ten minutes, which meant they probably put the cameras in everyday devices—smoke detectors, electrical outlets, stuffed teddy bears, edge of table tops, shelves. Listen as you walk through the place. Some hidden motion-sensing surveillance cameras make an almost inaudible buzz when in use."

Max chimed in. "Definitely don't make it obvious that you're looking. Pretend to clean up or something."

I nodded.

Xavier continued, "When I used to install shit like this for most guys, they never really loaded up the perp's bedroom or bathroom with cameras. Most wanted a focus on the living room. People do business in there. Meet with police and rival gangs in there. That's what these Russians are watching you for, making sure your ass doesn't get stupid and try to get help."

"Okay." I nodded. "You're right. Last time the Chinese didn't put anything in my bathroom or bedroom. That makes sense."

"Bathroom causes problems for surveillance. Your place has a small one too. Shower steam could fuck it up. If they put something there, it's in the door knob." Xavier made the sign of a cross. "If that knob hole now looks like a tiny cross opening in the center, there's a camera there."

I wrote everything down in my head.

"For the bedroom, turn off the lights." Xavier tapped the ash off his joint. "I used to install night vision security cameras for that shady hotel on Merker Street. Back in the day, when the owner like to have shit on people. Some creepy hotel managers still put a camera in their customers' rooms."

"That's fucking crazy." Maxell frowned.

"People are crazy." Xavier turned back to me. "Either way, all you do is turn off the lights, most hidden security cameras have red or green LEDs. The LEDs will blink or shine, when in low-light conditions."

"Anything else?" I asked.

"Yeah." Xavier glared at me. "Leave this whole situation alone."

"What do you want me to do? Darryl's my brother, I love him. I take care of him. Anybody can't get that, shouldn't be fucking with me."

Xavier rolled his eyes. "I don't invite you all to my happy abode, you two come over here bringing mess my way."

Max raised his hands. "Okay. Okay. Let's stay on track, guys."

I stirred. "I don't like them watching me. I want to do what we did with the Chinese and put a bug on the top guy—"

"Are you fucking crazy?" Max asked. "You want to track the leader."

"Yeah." I nodded. "He seems like the type to come into a person's place without knocking. The last thing I need is him sitting in my kitchen one morning when I wake up."

Xavier finished his joint. "That shit would be dangerous, if he ever found out."

"Then, we make sure he doesn't find out." I looked at Max. "Have you found anything on Kazimir?"

"Shit. Have I found anything on him?" Max laughed. "The motherfucker's reputation proceeds him. People call him the Russian Lion. I did a search and several FBI sites came up. He's considered the number seven most dangerous person in the world."

Fear hit my heart, but I pushed it away. "Well, at least he's not number one."

"He's suspected of heading Bratva which is involved in anything you can think of—diamond and arms dealing, credit card fraud, cybercrime, drugs, prostitution. Anything you can think of, his group does it."

"Group." Xavier laughed. "You make it sound like a club of dainty women. It's the fucking Russian mafia. They have no qualms about murdering people. If they have to kill you, they kill you."

Max continued, "He's not even supposed to be in America. There's a huge reward for any sighting or information on him, which is not an option for us because I bet he has FBI agents on his payroll—"

"And probably the NYPD," Xavier added. "There's no way Rumi committed suicide. The bastard loved himself too much. Sounds like dirty cops in the mix, covering shit up."

Max began to pace by the brick wall. "I think it's a good time to get out of here. We saved up some money. Let's just leave New York."

Max always wants to run. Scaredy cat.

It had taken him a month to walk through the tunnels without jumping at rats and screaming in fear. It was a whole year before he would even walk through them by himself, and even now he wasn't excited about taking them.

I shook my head. "We saved up twenty thousand. That's not shit for us to live on forever. Where are we going? We've never left New York. And, what are you going to do, be a bag boy at a grocery store?" I asked. "Our skills aren't resume-worthy. And besides, they have Darryl. I'm not leaving New York without Darryl."

"Darryl put himself into this shit." Xavier put the tiny burnt out joint in his pocket. "Why don't you let him get himself out."

Maxwell said nothing.

"We don't know if Darryl put himself in this or not, and it doesn't matter," I said. "He's my brother. I'll protect him to the end."

"I'm glad he's your brother because I'm not in this." Xavier rose from the steps and turned to go back inside his bus. "You both let me know how it works out, if you don't end up dead."

"X, I need you, please."

He kept his back to me. "What do you need?"

"Just a little tracker job."

"Don't even think about it," Max said. "If this Russian is hiding from the FBI and fucking Interpol, he would probably not appreciate someone tracking him."

"He started it," I said. "He probably has surveillance over my place. People probably went all in my apartment and touched my things. I just want to put something on him to keep track of where he is until this is done."

Xavier looked over his shoulder. "How do you want to track him?"

"I could probably grab his phone like we did with the Chinese."

When kids were hungry and alone on the streets, they picked up nifty skills like pickpocketing.

In my opinion, I was the best in New York. I could stand and talk to someone about normal conversation as I took my time taking their keys, wallet, and phone. It was all about distraction.

"Don't do this shit, Em," Max said. "Please."

"She won't listen." Xavier turned around. "But you know what? If your dumb behind can get that phone, bring it to me, and give me time to put a tracker in the battery, I'll do it. But that's it. Don't come over here for anything else."

Xavier always added that last line, but we knew it was bullshit. Xavier lost his daughters—my childhood friends. Not only did we remind him of them, we'd ended up being his children by chaotic default.

"How long would it take you to put the tracker in the battery?" I asked.

"Five minutes at the most." Xavier shut the bus door, ending out visit without a goodbye.

Maxwell looked at me. "How the hell are you going to take his phone?"

I shrugged.

"What are you going to do, when you get in the apartment?"

I shrugged again. "I'm pretty much going with what comes."

Max sighed. "Well, if you want my advice, which you probably don't...use your biggest weapon."

"What's that?"

"Sex appeal." He winked at me. "Seduce the lion."

My nerves frazzled a little at the thought. I didn't have a problem with flirting with men to get what I want or to remain safe. It was just that usually I wasn't attracted to the target which made it acting and nothing more.

With this Kazimir, I wasn't sure if I could keep my hormones from reacting.

"Don't overdo it. Just seize the opportunity for arousing him, when possible. Men are many things, but we aren't that complicated when it comes to women." Max walked off.

I followed. "So, what should I do with this one? I might not even be his type."

Max laughed. "When a woman's titties come out, she ends up being every man's type."

I paused in the alley.

He stopped and smiled at me. "You happen to have a nice rack."

I rolled my eyes. "So, your advice is to show him my breasts. It's that easy? He comes over and I'm like, 'Hey, check out my titties!'"

"No way." Max looked off in the direction of our building. "You know he has cameras in there, but he doesn't know you know that. First, figure out where all the cameras are and then give him a strip tease. Take off a little, but don't get naked. Keep it slow, making him want more. Show him no more than your bra and panties. Figure out where the camera is, turn around, take your bra off, put a shirt on, and then go to sleep. That should be enough."

"Do this tonight?"

"No, too soon. Let him pick you up tomorrow. Flirt with him. Put that feminine charm on him. Then, later that night...go for it."

"And then what?" I asked.

Maxwell gazed at our building. "We'll see."

"He might not be the one even looking at the cameras."

"True, but do you have any other options because if you do, take them. And if you're giving him that charm, he'll look." Max turned his attention to the full moon. "Have you heard from Kennedy?"

"No. Why?"

"I thought it was weird that she left."

"I didn't have time to think about it, being that I was dealing with a lion."

"Maybe, we should keep her out of this."

"I agree. This is a dirty situation anyway. No need to pull others in."

"Stay safe." Max saluted and headed away. "I've got something to check on. I'll see you later."

"Stay safe."

Max walked off in the other direction. Worry covered his face.

Find the cameras and seduce the lion? Easy. What could go wrong, but everything?

Chapter 6

Kazimir

The Russian Tea Room had satisfied my hunger.

The decor was wild with red and gold featured everywhere. Very ornate furnishings. There was even a giant glass bear filled with water that rotated in the center of the restaurant.

A couple whispered and sat at the table. Their hushed conversation reached to us.

"This is why we should leave, Jason." The woman shook her head and didn't even touch her food. "Between the shootings and this new serial killer. I don't know what to do."

"It will be okay, honey." He chewed his steak. "Drink some more of your wine."

"I'm tired of you saying that to me." She crossed her arms over her chest. "It's like you're oblivious to what's going on around us."

"The police will find the Tinder Killer."

"And if they don't."

"He's not even killing women."

"Sure, for now it's black men, but—"

The man dropped his fork next to his plate and scowled. "Just drank your damn wine, Sue."

She did as he asked.

I laughed to myself and returned to my food.

Sasha remained quiet most of our meal, drinking in his surroundings and eavesdropping on other's conversations.

When we finally finished dinner, my phone buzzed.

I answered on the third ring. "Yes?"

Luka was on the other line. Fear laced my number one's voice.

This can't be good.

Luka and I had done time together—broken bones and snapped necks together. I was not used to hearing him sound nervous.

"We have a problem," Luka said.

"What is it?"

"We've lost the washer."

I gripped the phone hard. "The new one?"

"Yes."

Where are you, Emily?

I tried to keep the anger out of my voice. "How the fuck did you lose her?"

"She closed the gallery and shut off the lights. We thought she would come out afterwards. She never did. We're in front of her house now."

"And someone is still watching the gallery?"

"Yes. We even broke in. She was gone."

"And you checked the cameras in her house?"

"Yes. No one's gone in and out, but us."

I groaned.

My little mysh, where are you? Already you're a tricky little creature?

"I'm sorry, boss. We'll have her, before the end of the night." Luka knew he'd fucked up. We had no time for slip ups, especially from a woman so small.

Tricky and smart just like a mouse. Where did you go?

I calmed myself down. "I know you'll find her, and when you do, bring her to me. I don't care where I'm at or what time it is."

You can be tricky with others, Emily, but not with me.

"Yes, sir."

I shut off the phone.

He'll find her. He won't disappoint.

Luka had been my cellmate for six months in Moscow's Matrosskaya Tishina prison. The Pre-trial Detention Center had been operating in northeastern Moscow since 1946.

Luka had an Asian appearance, with long flowing hair. Taller than most bastards. He reminded me a lot of 80s Soviet rock singer—effeminate, but scary as fuck. Luka had been doing five years for fraud conspiracy and smuggling. The cops knew he'd done more but couldn't prove it. That was why they'd thrown him into my cell. I'd been there for double murder and illegal arms trafficking.

We'd got along with ease. I'd told him about my plan of breaking out.

Excitement had blazed in his eyes. "How will we do it, Kazimir?"
I'd smiled. "We'll use a spoon."

And that was how I'd made my first escape from jail. I'd broken a hole in my cell ceiling with my spoon, taking my time, day-by-day. Weeks later, we tore through, climbed in a ventilation shaft, and found ourselves on the roof of the two-story cell blocks which adjoined the main fence. After that, it was nothing. We simply jumped from the roof onto the main fence, and from the fence we jumped out of the prison grounds, racing to freedom.

Before us, only three other prisoners had escaped from Matrosskaya Tishina. No one had been able to break out since Luka and me.

Luka will find Emily. There's no need to worry.

Sasha sipped his vodka and then looked at me. "What's wrong?"

"Our mouse has escaped."

"No, this is *your* mouse." Sasha shook his head. "Who did she outsmart?"

"Luka."

Shocked hit his eyes. "If she slipped by Luka, then she's more than we thought."

"We'll see by the end of the night." I clenched my jaw.

Sasha chuckled.

I frowned. "What?"

"I'm already liking her. Anyone that can rattle your nerves is a good person to have."

"Enjoy. Emily will be found and brought to me, and then she'll understand that she is to go where I say and only breathe when I allow it."

"I don't know, Kazimir. These Harlem women—"

"She's a survivor and smart. She'll do as she's told because it'll depend on her life."

"I hope you're right." Sasha smirked. "If you're wrong, you should give her to me to kill."

"No."

We left the restaurant and he continued to keep that tickled expression on his face.

"What, Sasha?" I asked.

"Your sister told me that even when you were a little boy, you would hide the rats from everyone and feed them cheese."

"I had to hide them. They would've eaten them."

I got into the limo.

Pissed, I hid it well.

There weren't many times, when someone acted out of order. All knew to respect me, and what would happen, if they didn't. I'd assumed Emily was smarter than that. Surely, she understood that there would only be two options for her after my request—wash my money or die.

I don't want to kill you, mysh. Be good and pop up.

It took us twenty minutes later to get to the brothel that Rumi frequently used. I didn't know we'd still had brothels in America. My empire expanded across the globe. It was difficult to remember all the tiny ways we made money.

However, Sasha explained that Penelope's business was new and one of Sasha's personal hobbies that he'd started in New York. More pleasure than business.

We entered the building and stopped at the elevator.

My phone rang.

I had to admit, relief hit me, when Luka's name flashed on the screen.

He better have found her? Where could she have gone?
I placed the phone at my ear. "Yes?"
"We found her."
Good.
But, my frown never left my face. "Where did you find her?"
Luka cleared his throat as if not proud of himself. "She just appeared and walked up to the front door."
I raised my eyebrows. "She appeared from where?"
"My men think she came out of an alley a few blocks down."
A low growl lathered the word. "Think? They don't know?"
"Yes, sir. When we asked her how she'd gotten here, she simply said that it was a nice night out for a walk and she'd taken *the long way*. But sir. . .we have men everywhere. Other gangs, cops—"
"I'm aware of what we have."
"No one spotted her."
I stifled my groan of annoyance. This wasn't happening how it usually did. Washers remained out in the open and in my little cage—no matter how beautiful it was. They lived behind the bars and was transparent with all their steps. These were people that had their hands-on millions and millions of my dollars. Never should they disappear and reappear at will.
"Bring her to me." I gritted my teeth and shut off the phone.
Luka could get the address from our driver. I was too aggravated to talk to him further.
I placed the phone in my pocket as Sasha and I stepped on the elevator.
Sasha wore a smirk. "Has the mouse been found?"
"Yes."
The elevator doors closed.
"She'll be joining us here?" he asked.
"Yes."
"She's made you grumpy. Now you'll be no fun."

"Don't worry," I said. "Scaring her will brighten my mood."

"Try not to scare her too much."

It was a nice night for a walk, and she took the long way? Very clever. Too clever.

At least the brothel didn't disappoint.

Dim lighting kept the space in shadows. Soft music played in the background—something moody with a woman whispering in French. There were red and dark blue couches were tucked into corners. Large, framed, black-and-white photographs hung on the walls, showing rich images of sex—nude couples in dark colored silhouettes.

Beside the bouncers and bartenders, the rest of the staff were women, wearing tight leather pants and red silk halter tops. And the women that were there to serve. . .gorgeous, exotic, and probably deadlier than the men who paid them.

"Yes." I studied the place. "This has you written all over it, Sasha."

We sat down at one of small walnut tables at the back of the living room which was a space five times the size of a family room.

Before I could turn to the bartender, a tumbler of vodka appeared in front of me.

I smiled at the waitress, setting it down. "Hmmm. I like our new place already."

"Good." Sasha smiled which didn't happen much. "This is one of my pride and joys. I get a lot of information here. Men say anything to women, when their dicks are out. I let Penelope start this about two years ago."

"Even with technology and terrorism reshaping the crime world, sex still sells."

"There's always money in pussy." He gestured to a few of the beautiful women lounging on the couches in front of us. "Unlike the other brothels are women aren't trafficked. Happy pussy delivers better service."

I cheered his shot glass. "I've always found that to be true."

"These girls came for the American Dream and are paying off their trip. Already, some have gone on to marry and be small stars. You must see the rooftop. There is a section where there is always live sex and a band."

So Sasha.

I took another sip of the vodka. "And Alayna—our scout—she works here?"

"Yes." Sasha nodded. "This was where Darryl bragged to her. I don't know why he would try to impress a hooker. The only thing that makes one smile is money."

"Apparently, he had a way to get a lot of money."

"He says it was just a lie for pussy."

"I think it's bullshit." I finished the vodka. "He's still hiding something."

"You shot him with a nail gun. I imagine he's confessed it all."

"No. My gut says there's something more. I may talk to him later."

"No." Sasha sneered and shook his head. "Let me. I have my ways."

I thought of Emily. "No. Let's wait. I want him kept safe."

The waitress returned with a tray of high-end cigars. I shook my head, ignoring the I'm-down-to-fuck invitation in her gaze. Everyone wanted to fuck the boss, but no one understood the danger of my bed. Not every woman could handle the fact that my enemies would slit their necks just because they were close to me.

Too many of my brothers' wives and girlfriends had been killed. Therefore, I kept it simple. I got my cock wet, when the urge came. After a good orgasm, I continued the game of ruling the world.

Sasha finished his drink and fixed his blueish-gray gaze on me. "What's your plan for this evening?"

The waitress returned and filled my glass with more vodka. This time she made a show of displaying her full cleavage in that red halter top. It was nice, but what cleavage wasn't?

"What's my plan?" I turned back to Sasha. "The same. Find out who killed Rumi. I like the look of this Emily. I would rather her not have intestines hanging around her neck too."

"Fair point. Whoever killed Rumi would kill her."

"Which is why I like that she is under the radar. No one would think I would go to her for help."

"But, she does have a reputation."

"Yes, but with no one on our level," I said.

"I don't know. She slipped out of Luka's eyesight." Sasha wagged his finger. "That makes me nervous."

"Nervousness isn't so bad. It's just life telling you that shit is about to happen."

"Let's just hope it's good shit."

"It will be." I scanned the space and rose from the table. My men and Sasha stood too. I adjusted my jacket and smiled. "So, let's get a tour of your new little hobby. I also want to talk to Penelope."

Sasha smiled. "I figured you would."

The walk would clear my head and talking to Penelope about the missing hooker would ease my nerves. I had to keep busy while I considered what I would do with Emily.

She'll have to tell me how she did it. I don't like my washers haing secrets.

Sasha led me around, knowing every turn and door to go through. His ease of the place told me that he'd spent more time at this place than I'd understood. While I knew he'd gone to New York once a year, it must've been even more.

Interesting. It appears there are a lot of secrets going around tonight.

The brothel was set in a massive penthouse—a true palace in the sky with private elevators.

Above the penthouse was a rooftop garden and sky-high pool illuminated in a haunting blue. Naked women of all races and sizes lounged by the water as top ranked criminals swam around them or stood in the corner talking business with another.

The lushness of the place continued. There was glass curtain walls and barrel-vaulted ceilings. Velvet upholstery mingled with custom-designed furniture.

"Penelope's office is in the back." Sasha gestured that way. "We should talk to her now."

"Good."

We passed several rooms. Four of my men followed behind us, ready to shoot, slice, or choke anyone that came near. But no one would. Everyone was too busy fucking.

I had no idea how many bedrooms the penthouse had, but at least seven. Dim lighting and moans filled the journey to the madam's office. Erotic art hung on the walls of the passageway.

Sasha stopped at the last door in the hallway. "She spends most of her time in here, only coming out for the big spenders."

"And we're not big spenders?" I asked.

"She didn't know we were arriving, although I'm sure someone told her when we walked in." He knocked.

No answer came.

Sasha knocked again. After a few seconds, he turned the knob and opened the door.

The door widened.

The stench hit us first.

What is going on, New York?

A woman hung from the chandelier by her own intestines and wire. Dried blood caked her legs, gut, and neck. Long blonde hair fell to her waist. Diamonds decorated her neck, fingers, and wrists, although most of the jewelry had been splattered in blood. She'd been dangling there for a while.

The person did it the way Sasha would have.

Sasha hated blood—the scent, the feel, the sight. Even when he killed, he did so in clean ways—ropes, needles, drowning, etc.

Sasha grinned at the killer's handiwork. "Beautiful. Don't you think?"

"This is Penelope?" I asked.

"It was."

I didn't enter the office.

I'd found my mother dead in her bed, surrounded by all those furs. I'd sat next to her lifeless body and cried. It was the only time I could ever remember crying. Nevertheless, female corpses were the only ones I didn't like to walk up on. They reminded me of Mom.

Yet, Sasha walked in with sick intrigue in his eyes. "What is it with this guy and intestines?"

I avoided looking at Penelope. By this time, Sasha was so close to her that he'd get the necessary information.

Shaking my head, I turned my attention to the pool of dried blood under her body. "She's been dead since this morning?"

"Yes." Sasha slowly circled her and then touched her hand. "Cold and hard. She probably died an hour or so after Rumi."

"Someone was cleaning up loose ends."

"Yes. Penelope must've known something."

My washer and now the brothel owner. Who is doing this? And where is the missing hooker?

I raised my eyebrows. "Who will run this brothel now?"

"Alayna. I trust her."

"Me too." I gestured to one of my men. "Take care of this. No one needs to know. But first call a couple cops to get prints and investigate. I want to know who did it by tomorrow."

I turned away, done with all the death I'd seen so far. Whoever thought they could kill my people with ease would find out soon what I was capable of. And I wouldn't just hurt the people involved, I would kill their families first—right in front of them—just to hear their screams.

Surprises. Too many fucking surprises. I hate coming to this country.

My phone rang.

This time Luka texted, probably done with hearing my annoyance.

Luka: We are in the lounge room. Where should I take her?

Me: To the roof top.

Luka: Yes, sir.

Sasha had taken me up there, but it had been a quick tour. I'd been too eager to question Penelope about her missing hooker. But now I needed air to think. Dealing with Emily under the stars would be just the thing I needed to put me back on track.

I put the phone up.

Sasha got to my side. "The mouse is here?"

"Yes." I gestured to the room. "Sasha, it appears this problem may be bigger than I thought. You wanted control. Here it is. Find out what happened to Penelope."

Sasha leaned his head to the side. "Are you sure you won't need help with your mouse? I can help there too."

"No. I have her."

"She may disappear, before you get to her. Where is she?"

"I told Luka to take her to the rooftop."

"The roof? Interesting. Where the live sex performance is?" He chuckled. "I know what you're doing. You're pushing her out of her comfort zone, keeping her on edge."

"I thought I'd done it in her office, but she was never nervous enough."

"Enjoy your rooftop meeting." Sasha pointed to the room. "I'll deal with Penelope's killer."

Chapter 7
Emily

What the hell are they going to do to me?

The Russians didn't seem pleased with my tunnel run. When I showed up, they didn't even let me change. They carted me off to a car and drove me away. I was now at some freaky sex place, completely exposed—no wig, no identity to slip on and off. They made me come just as I was—Emily from Harlem. Cornrows, jeans, sneakers, and my lucky black jacket.

Kazimir would meet the true me, and I wasn't happy about it at all.

I'll have to be more careful next time, only slip away when it's an emergency.

If Kazimir thought he was going to completely control me, he'd be in for a big surprise. I would rather die, then be trapped. Sure, I would wear his doggy leash if he needed. I'd jump, when he asked and run, when he ordered. Anything to keep Darryl safe. But I wouldn't be watched for too long, and no one—not even him and his scary men—would know my moves and secrets.

A burly man had been escorting me since they'd found me.

"Let's go." He grabbed my hand, rough calloused scratched my fingers, but it was better than ramming a gun in my face—something he'd been threatening to do if I disappeared again.

I didn't waste my time, asking where we were going. It wasn't like I had a decision in it. Talking was a distraction. I found it best to keep my mouth closed and eyes open in situations like this.

He led him lead me through this luxury penthouse like a child. Sweat beaded at his forehead. Him losing me must've been a total fuck up. It would be a good idea not to push his nerves even further, so instead I kept his pace and drank in the scene around me. I had no idea what Kazimir had in store. I might need to know how to get out of here on my own.

But my burly bodyguard rushed us through everything. I didn't get a chance to really take the place in. It was obviously filled with prostitutes. Either this was how Russians partied, when they came to New York to visit or this was a sex business. I didn't know the place, but it was high-end and with an exclusive Manhattan location which meant that my level of people didn't frequent here.

This was a spot for bosses of bosses to relax.

I swallowed. Just the knowledge of this location could get me killed, if I wasn't careful and kept my mouth closed.

We went upstairs and reached another hallway. The smell of cigars and sex coated the air. Three half naked women laughed and ran away from a big belled man with nothing on either. Seconds later, they passed by us. Water covered their bodies like they'd just jumped out of the pool.

We paused in front of a door.

My bodyguard whispered to a huge man stepping in front. They engaged in a hushed, yet heated conversation.

What the fuck is going on?

I glanced back. In a shadowed corner, an old man in a suit sat on a crimson velvet couch. A petite blonde had her face buried in his crotch. He must've had his pants open. His eyes remained closed as his hand rested on the back of her head, guiding it up and down.

My heart beats increased. I knew I should look away, but I leaned back to catch the thick accented words leaving his parted mouth.

"Just like that." He guided her head down, opened his eyes, and stared at me. "Yes. Take it all the way to the back of your throat."

Slurping noises rose from her.

Still watching me, he smiled. "Swallow it all."

My bodyguard nudged my elbow. "Come."

This night keeps getting crazier and crazier.

I left the blow job show and followed my guard through the door.

I spotted the rooftop pool first.

Damn. This isn't a penthouse. It's a mansion on top of a building.

The full moon hung in the sky. It was a breezy night. Almost everyone was naked around and in the pool. The pool must've been heated. Steam rose from the rippling surface and some of the women's nude bodies.

I kept my head low. I didn't want to know who was here, and I didn't want anyone to know me either. Still, many men looked my way. A few whispered to the women.

For one minute, I wondered if Kazimir would be meeting me naked and in the middle of two giggling, big-breasted prostitutes. For some reason, that thought gave me a bad taste. He seemed too cool and full of swag to hang out in a place like this, chasing after naked women like many of the old, out-of-shape men that sat around the pool.

God, I hope he has clothes on. I need to be focused.

Without clothes, I was sure he'd be layers of muscle and probably a long, hard cock. He damn sure walked like he had a big one.

Stop thinking about his cock, and just get out of here.

We left the pool area, and to my surprise the roof continued.

Another door appeared made of blue and red glass.

My bodyguard dropped my hand and opened the door for me. "Go in. I'll be here."

What?

I stepped inside. "Where will he be?"

The man closed the door as if completely done with me and my antics for the evening.

Jesus! I just wanted to take a walk by myself before I started working for you. I was barely gone for an hour.

I sighed and walked further in. Walls had been built around the outline of the roof, converting the space into a large room with the sky as the ceiling. Soft, sensual music played in the background. Every light was dimmed to a muted glow. There was something growing in the air—thick an animalistic. Hunger decorated everyone's faces as they stare at something in the center of the room.

Where are you, Kazimir?

Several leather couches of varying lengths as well as large armchairs dotted the space. Torches stood in the corners.

I did a quick count of the room. There were only twenty people inside. Men and women. The ages fell between early twenties to sixties. Many wore tuxedoes and expensive dresses. Some men had women perched on their laps, hands casually fondling breasts or sliding between parted legs. Others leaned against the walls or crowded into the corners, their grunts and low cries sprinkling the air. Every person was transfixed on something happening at the center of the room.

Walking further to see what they saw, my gaze found the focal point.

Oh wow.

The music shifted to a darker more erotic beat. Something I would love to fuck to but would never listen to as I was walking down the street. The song was slow, yet the beat grew, inciting images of sex to play out in my head.

At the center of the room there was a naked couple on a bed surrounded by a glass box. A dark skinned muscular man toyed between a red head's thighs. His long dreadlocks fell to the bed. Had he been standing, the locs might've fallen to his waist—a very muscular one too. The woman had small breasts, a slim frame, and no hair anywhere else besides her head.

And her reddish-brown hair falls in waves around her face down to the middle of her arched back. From my view, she has these honey-colored eyes that look like liquid gold. She was curvy and plump.

They were probably in their early twenties like me. Yet, they were both utterly beautiful—moving art. Fluid. Erotic. Both enrapt in passion with the other. She moved like a sensual dancer, rolling her body with his in time with the song's erotic beat. The tempo drummed in my chest, almost in sync with the couple.

This is the last place I need to be.

Caught in a trance, I stepped forward, not even sure how far I'd walked. I just needed a closer look of them.

Where is Kazimir?

Had Kazimir asked around about me *that* much? He'd certainly found the right people to talk to. Had they clued him in on my sexual life—maybe the fact that some thought I was an addict—a freak, hoe, slut, fast girl. It was all rumors and whisperings of resentful men. Mad that they couldn't keep my attention for longer than a week. Pissed that I'd hopped in another the next. Dick hurt that I never answered their calls begging me back.

If Kazimir had asked around, he might've discovered that sex could be a weak point with me—something he could possibly use. I wasn't sure, if I had a problem with sex or not. I loved it. Sometimes I had to have it and nothing else would matter until that rush had been fixed. Most of the time it didn't matter. And then other times, the urge for sex came at high-anxiety times and I couldn't breathe unless I had someone moving over me, pumping the stress away.

I moved closer, passing the beautifully dressed people on the couches. No one looked my way. Everyone was captivated with the couple having sex.

And like the audience, I turned back to the couple.

Hovering over the red-head, the man lapped at her pink nipple.

"Yes," she cried out and arched her back.

The man slid his large hand down her flat stomach. His fingers disappeared between her legs, stroking bare flesh, already glistening with moisture. Without releasing her nipple from his mouth, he spread her thighs wider, pressing them flat to the bed so the audience had a perfect, erotic view of his thick fingers sliding through her flushed, pink lips and dipping into her pussy.

Even through the glass partition, her cry of pleasure reached us.

A shudder rippled through my body as a tiny moan left my lips.

Fuck. Get it together. I'm not here for this. I'm here to deal with Kazimir.

I gulped in a fresh breath of air and scanned the place for Kazimir and couldn't find him.

Moans filled the air in front of me.

Gritting my teeth, I refused to look their way.

Where are you?

And then I turned around, and he stood directly behind me. I tensed. How long had he been watching my reaction to the couple? Had he heard the tiny moans that left my mouth? How long had he watched me soak all the sex in?

The couple was now behind me, where they had to stay. There was no way I could watch them and focus on Kazimir.

Is that what you planned? If so, good move.

He studied me, letting his gaze fall on my sneakers, rise my jeans, jacket, and landed on my swirling cornrow.

That thick Russian accent layered his words. "I like your hair. It's so different than anything I've seen before."

Okay. I wasn't expecting that.

"Yes," the red head behind me moaned.

Kazimir raised his hand to my head, touched one of my tiny cornrows with his finger, and trailed the whole swirled path, slipping along the top of my head, twisting and turning in the back, and falling past my shoulder. "Stunning."

"Thank you?" I hadn't meant to sound so unsure, but he'd been the one to have his men drag me to a rooftop with sex on it. I didn't think we'd be talking about my hairstyle.

"You changed your hair fast."

"I was wearing a wig before."

"I see." He nodded and slowly walked a circle around me. "You looked like a top art gallery owner earlier. Only a few hours later, you look like you would break into that same gallery. . .but with finesse and style." He walked around again and stood behind me. His breath brushed the back of my neck. "You're still so beautiful, but now the danger isn't so hidden like before."

It was in that moment, I noticed several suited men come in. Couple by couple the men signaled for the audience to leave.

Why are you clearing the room?

Stepping back in front of me, Kazimir didn't look put off by the emptying roof, which told me the men worked under his orders.

Meanwhile, the naked couple remained in the center. Their moans rose in the air. The bed creaked with the rhythm of their groans and shudders.

I blinked, my nipples getting hard under my shirt. Thank God I still had on my jacket. Of all the people to get rid of, the ones having sex would've been my first choice.

But that was the thing about men like Kazimir. They dominated the world because they learned a person's weakness fast and used them against the person. It was the main reason why I wore disguises—always keeping people guessing.

A hard expression covered Kazimir's face. I immediately missed his smile. At least in the gallery, he seemed like a reasonable man.

Now? Not so reasonable.

He remained in front of me as the last audience member left.

I inched back.

He raised part of his lip into a sneer and closed most of the distance between us. Barely leaving an inch of space.

I didn't move.

He pierced me with an intense gaze. "Where did you go?"

I swallowed in my fear. "I took the alleys."

"No. My men would've seen you."

"I'm born and raised here. Harlem runs through my veins like blood—"

"Still, you didn't take the alleys."

I tried not to blink. Something about bad guys and not blinking made them think I was telling the truth. But that didn't work with Kazimir.

I could tell him about the tunnels, but then if I needed to escape from him, the tunnels wouldn't be an option.

I'm not telling you where I went.

"I'm sorry." I gazed at the floor. "I won't ever go missing again."

"So, you do admit you intentionally went missing?"

I tapped my fingers against my thighs. "I'm sorry. It had nothing to do with your men...not completely. I just like my privacy."

"That's closer to the truth."

What's giving me away? Usually, no one can tell, when I'm lying.

The couple moaned some more behind me. The bed creaked. My body came alive. My panties moistened. I tried my best to look unaffected.

Don't let him see. Stay calm and relaxed.

"Fuck me," the red head moaned, "Give me that big cock."

I held in my moan.

"Hmmm." Kazimir leaned my way and breathed me in as if catching my horny scent like a hound dog, giving him the ability to track me forever. My cheeks warmed.

The couple and him turned me on. Maybe it was the danger radiating off Kazimir's perfect face. Perhaps it was the fact that he looked mad, but not enough to sling me off the roof. And I was so grateful...so grateful I would have loved to give him some.

Stop it. Stop it. Stop it.

This was bad. The moonlight wouldn't hide the fact that my eyes were probably dilated with lust.

"Little *mysh*," he whispered, and I wondered what that word meant.

I hope mysh means "Hey, we're friends again."

He brought those cold eyes to me and gave me a wicked smile. "You like your privacy?"

"Yes."

"Turn around."

Damn it. No. I don't want to see the sex.

Regardless, I did as he ordered, putting the live sex right in front of me.

Within the glassed-box, the dreadlocked man now thrusted into the red-head. The man's sculpted ass flexed as he stroked. It was beautiful. Two lush bodies sliding and moving together. Completely erotic and dripping with sensuality.

Fuck.

My nipples tightened almost in pain, not understanding why they couldn't get in on the fun. I inched backward into Kazimir, and it felt good to be so close.

Fuck. I'm too horny for this.

I got ready to step away.

Gripping my hips, he moved closer, pressing his chest to my back. The thickness of his cock pushed the high rise of my ass and the dip in my spine.

I wasn't foolish enough to think his erection was for me. There was plenty of reason for him to be turned on in a brothel. But still, his cock pressed into my ass, and there was no doubting the size and power.

I tensed, unsure of how to act or what to say. Never had I experienced this before. Many gangsters had tried to dominate me, but none had done it with sex. They did it with yelling and threats, even guns pointed right at my face.

But this method, I didn't know what to do with.

How did he know this would knock me off balance?

Kazimir didn't try to hide the erection as he whispered against my ears, "You like your privacy, but you don't get privacy with me."

His words should've thrown me on edge, but with the sex in front and his hard body behind, I felt sandwiched between lust. I yearned to fuck—anybody—at that moment.

Kazimir—of course—was at the top of the list.

"You're too important to me now." He moved in closer, letting his front mold into my back. "Do you understand?"

"Yes." I shuddered, melting into the hard contours of his chest.

And the damn sexy couple continued to play their sensual scene in front of them. Her chest rose and fell on rapid breaths as the man gave her long strokes, rocking his hips and clenching his muscled ass.

My panties moistened more. I yearned for Kazimir to touch me and slide his hands up my body, cupping my breasts. My shoulders rose and fell with my labored breaths, anticipating the feel of his hands on my body.

"You want to hide from me, Emily?" His words danced down the curve of my neck, delivering tingles along the sensitive flesh. "But we're friends."

He placed both of his hands on my hips. "Friendships take time and energy to grow."

My heart hammered in my chest. My nipples pebbled in pleasurable pain.

"Do you understand now, Emily?"

I didn't mean to, but I moaned my answer, "Yes."

Gripping my hips harder, he breathed me in.

"Very dangerous." He brushed his lips against my ear.

And then to my surprise, Kazimir stepped away.

What?

I should've waited for his order, but I turned around in time to catch him, running his fingers through his hair with desire blazing in his eyes.

Fuck. Maybe this isn't just about dominance. He looks ready to fuck me too.

I really wanted to look down at his cock, but I forced myself to remain straight with a neutral expression. There was no need for him to know how much he was affecting me.

Silent, he gazed at me for too long, shoving me off edge.

I felt naked in front of him.

"Hmmm." He raised one hand in the air and snapped his fingers.

The couple's moans stopped behind me. There was shuffling and rustling. Minutes later, the nude couple scurried out of there too.

Kazimir and I were the only two people left in the moonlit place.

Even his guards were on the other side of the wall.

Finally, he cut the silence. "The man that brought you here will be your personal guard. His name is Luka."

I don't need a damn guard! But. . .you didn't ask so. . .I'll just keep that to myself.

"You're too smart." He placed his hands in his suit pants. "You disappear within minutes. Change looks within seconds. Too smart."

It was just a wig. I'm not the Master of Disguises.

As if he heard me, he responded, "It doesn't matter. Luka will sit in your living room, when you're home. And when you're working, he'll be in the gallery's lobby. And when you want to take a nice *long wak*, he'll be right beside you, helping you enjoy the sunny day. Think of him as your shadow."

I murmured, "Okay."

"We're friends, Emily." He curved those wicked lips into a smile. "It would make me feel more comfortable, if you were safe at all times."

"I understand. I'll do anything to make you feel more comfortable."

To my surprise, he licked his lips.

Not the reaction I thought I would get, but. . .okay.

He slipped his gaze down the front of my jacket as if his eyes could open the garment. But then, maybe it was all my imagination because I surely wanted him to open it.

No. He's too dangerous for a fling.

He raised his eyebrows. "Do you have any questions?"

I was surprised he'd even asked.

Well. . .I'm horny now, thanks for that. So. . .I'll probably do a quick hook up from Tinder. Where does Luka hang out during my sexy times? Will he be sitting in one corner of the bed watching?

I shifted my weight to one foot, trying to figure out a way to ask him.

"Say it," Kazimir said. "You definitely have a question on your mind."

"When I'm. . .on a date with a guy, will Luka still have to be with me?"

"Let's leave that question for when you have time for dating." Kazimir shrugged. "For now, you simply don't have the time. Our new arrangement will keep you busy."

And how long will this new arrangement last? How long will you have my brother?

Before I could ask, he glared at me. "Don't disappear again."

I nodded.

"Being my washer has become a dangerous job," he continued, "It would be smart to be with my men the whole time."

"Of course."

"Besides, there's talk of a serial killer in the city." He studied my face again and then turned his attention to my braids. "I really like your hair this way."

And with that, he left me on the roof top, horny and in shock.

Okay. I'm still alive, and he's even more dangerous than I thought.

And I didn't know what had knocked me off balance the most, his orders, the sex on the roof, or the fact that he'd pressed his cock to my behind and never offered more.

Damn. Thank God he hadn't. I don't know if I could say no.

I was supposed to be the one seducing Kazimir, not the other way around.

Had Maxwell been around, he would've been shaking his head.

"Never let the gangsters get the upper hand, Em"

Well, that rule had been easier to follow, when the gangsters looked like crap. But Kazimir was gorgeous. I imagined many women had difficulty keeping their clothes on around him.

I must get the upper hand. He's supposed to be hot for me, not the other way around.

Walking off the roof with Luka on my right, I wondered how I could turn everything back around.

Chapter 8

Kazimir

When I entered my bedroom, the woman from the live sex performance on the roof was now on my bed. She was red hair and honey colored eyes. Breathtaking. Gorgeous. Beautiful.

Not enough. Not tonight.

"Did you enjoy my performance?" She slipped her hands along the silky red dress she wore that matched her hair perfectly.

Sasha and I had decided to stay in the same building as the brothel just in case something else came up.

I studied the woman as she smiled back at me. "Yes, I enjoyed your performance."

There was no reason to ask why she was there. Sasha knew I would want to stuff my cock into something after running around Harlem all day. My body surely needed the release. And who else, but the best of our establishment to please me?

But the problem was that I needed another type of creature this evening and she'd just walked away from me.

"You are beautiful," I said to the woman on the bed. "But tonight, I will not need you."

Frowning, she rose from the bed and swayed over to me. "And tomorrow night?"

"That is a question for tomorrow."

She reached out to touch my lips.

I gently grabbed her hand, before she could. "Goodnight."

She put on a fake smile, but her eyes said she was aggravated.

"I guess that is a goodnight." She moved her hand and walked around me. "I will see you later."

I never turned around as the door closed behind me.

How did Emily escape Luka?

I smiled at the absurdity of it all. Such a beautiful, yet soft woman bypassing a big scary man like Luka.

What is she doing now? Did the rooftop talk teach her a lesson?

I'd used a different method with Emily. I'd intended the sex to make her uncomfortable, but she'd shifted to the opposite—completely turned on and damn near licking her lips at the sight of the fucking couple. I'd watched her feet move a centimeter and her thighs press together and knew she was getting wet.

My cock surely yearned to teach her more. I'd planned to dominate her, yet her body had lured me in for something more. To my destruction, I'd gotten too close. So close, I swore I could smell the sweet scent of her pussy as we talked.

Who dominated who on the roof tonight?

It had shifted my goals. I'd gone from wanting to teach her a lesson to yearning to bend her over and show the couple and her what real sex looked like.

But it was just a consequence of the moment. Nothing else. The brothel reeked of sex. The couple had ignited the need for lust higher and damn near had sprayed hormones into the audience. I'd enjoyed watching the couple, but when Emily stepped into the space, for some reason, I'd enjoyed watching her more.

And it was the way she gazed at the sex going on in front of her that made my cock hard. It had caught me by surprise. Her eyes were transfixed. She'd become intoxicated—eyes dilated, her teeth constantly capturing her lips. And when I pressed my cock against that soft ass, she didn't rush away instantly, she lingered. So much that, when she finally decided to step away, I couldn't deal with the space between us.

My little mysh.

I sat on my bed and checked my laptop on the night stand.

Ivan had set up everything as I ordered, placing a continuous feed of the cameras in Emily's apartment. Six boxes played on the screen. I pressed on the box where she'd moved in.

The camera's view largened to full screen.

Like me, Emily was on her bed. Exhaustion covered her face.

A queen bed stood on the other side of the room. Moonlight spilled into her bedroom from a large window.

The room appeared tight and cramped.

Ivan had delivered a pdf file of her blueprints. The two-bedroom apartment was less than a few thousand square feet. The other bedroom was bigger. For some reason Emily had chosen the smallest space to sleep in.

Why and why do I care?

She lay on her side. The curve of her hip stuck up under a small blanket. I yearned to run my hands over that arc to her waist. Such a simple pose, yet I licked my lips and imagining me spooning her from her behind and her thickness molded against my body.

Sighing, she moved the blanket off her and sat up.

Can't go to sleep?

I swore she frowned and glanced up at the ceiling, right at the camera.

No. She doesn't know I'm watching her.

She crossed her arms over her chest, barely hiding those full breasts. The simple gesture made me horny.

"Take the shirt off, *mysh*."

I bet her bra overflowed with those full breasts. If I'd been in the room, I would've had her undress. I'd cup those lush mounds, pinching and plucking her nipples. I grunted as I titty fucked her in my mind. That soft bosom cushioning my hard cock as I slipped the hungry length between them.

Knocking my dirty thoughts away, she muttered to herself. "He started it."

Who started it, mysh?

A little bit of annoyance hit me. She was a free woman? This man should've been none of my concern. Shaking my head, I tried to stop the desire that's rushed through me. Now was not the time to lose my head.

Slowly, she took off her sneakers.

What are you thinking about?

She stood up and turned away from the camera. I had that feeling again that she might've known I was watching her.

She probably does. She's proven to be smart.

I licked my lips as she raised her shirt and pulled it off. Next, she unsnapped her bra and placed it on the bed. Her bare back greeted my eyes.

I touched the tips of my fingers to the computer screen, wishing I could trail them down Emily's soft skin. It had to be silky. Dandelion soft. High end silk.

A tree covered her entire back. I inched closer staring at the large tattoo. There was beauty in the lines. Three black birds flew over the branches right near the back of her right shoulder. The trunk grew along her spine. The roots dipped down into her jeans, and the branches spread out to the sides, and I craved to touch each one, tracing them with my finger.

Why the tree, Emily?

Tattoos were significant in my world. Especially when it came to the jail system. If an inmate had a dagger through the neck it meant that he'd murdered before and was available to be hired. A cross on the chest symbolized a loyalty to fellow thieves. Others wore the Madonna and Child to ward off evil.

When Sasha had gone to prison, he'd made too many enemies. Men had held him down and tattooed eyes on his stomach. It was a common way among inmates to mark if a person was gay. When Sasha gained strength, those men died and their brothers outside of prison living normal lives, they were killed too. And Sasha slit their throats and cut eyes on their chests.

Tattoos meant a lot in my world.

What does the tree mean to you, Emily?

With her back still to me, she placed her hands on the top of her jeans. Impatiently, I waited for her to slip them down, needing to see something—anything of her. But she froze there for a few minutes as if thinking, if she should or shouldn't.

Yes. You know I'm watching. Don't you?

Instead of taking off her jeans, she hugged her breasts, hiding them with her arms.

"*Kakogo chyorta*," I muttered under my breath. "You could've shown me something, after the mess you got yourself into tonight."

Turning off her bedroom's lights, she walked off to her bathroom, entered, and closed the door.

Yet, that tattoo from her back remained in my head. She'd picked a tree and for some reason I needed to know why. The damn image haunted me.

An old memory hit my head.

"*A tattoo is not just body art.*" Uncle Igor sat in front of Luka and I, holding his adapted electric shaver in his hand. On his chest was a double headed eagle, gripping a heavy cross in his talons. "*A tattoo tells a story about the person wearing it. It is a tale of the soul. What do you want?*"

I showed him my arm. "A lion."

"*And you Luka?*" Uncle Igor pulled out needles from his draw and an ampoule of liquid dye.

"*A bear on the front of my chest.*"

"*You two escaped a place that many haven't. Everyone's talking about it.*" Uncle Luka twisted the adapted electric razor in his hand. "*This will change your lives. Stay close to each other. Trust no one. Not even those that claim to be your blood.*"

I nodded.

Uncle Igor pierced me with a haunted gaze. "Look to everything around you for a sign. You are guided by something more, Kazimir. There will always be enemies around you."

Uncle Igor turned on the razor to start my tattoo. "The ones that are special. The ones that seemed blessed. Hold on to them, but do not cage them. They're supposed to live in the sky."

When I'd come into power, Uncle Igor placed the traditional eight-pointed stars on my collarbones.

What did a tree mean for her?

On the screen, Emily's shower sounded from the closed door.

Sighing, I undressed, turned off the light, and climbed into bed.

I had a capable, warm woman right in my room and I told her to leave. And instead of fucking someone, I'm staring at the damn computer, hoping my washer will show her tits. What the fuck am I doing?

It had been a long flight and an even longer day. Emily was supposed to be the easiest part of the trip, but for some reason she'd aggravated me more than the brothel madam's and Rumi's deaths.

Emily was supposed to stay where she was put. All signs pointed to that action being logical. Surely, she'd feared me. Instead she risked a few moments of *privacy.*

Where had she really gone? Should I have pushed her for more answers?

I gritted my teeth. It was unlike me to second guess my actions, especially when it came to a woman. Had it been a man, I might've flung him off the roof. With her, I'd hesitated.

It had been those damn eyes. Closed off, not telling me anything.

I thought back to the tattoo again right as the sound of the shower turning off came from the laptop. My room was dark, except for the moonlight streaming in through my curtains and the light from the computer screen.

I turned to my side and lay under the covers naked as I always did. But tonight, was different. Usually, I didn't lay in bed alone, and never did I stare at my laptop, hoping for one of my workers to show me more.

She opened the door. A large towel wrapped around her.

My cock jerked against my thigh.

I'm probably going to fuck you, Emily.

She stood in the doorway but didn't gaze up to the camera.

With her light off in the bedroom and only dim lightening coming from her bathroom, all I could really make out was a sexy silhouette.

Everything in me, yearned to see more.

And for the first time in years, I slipped my hand down to my cock and squeezed the tip. It had been a long time since I'd ever needed to stroke my own cock. Women waited patiently by the phone for me in many countries. Even now I could've ordered three or four from the brothel right above me.

Yet, Emily stood in the doorway—a sexy silhouette in a towel—and I rubbed the long length of my cock, pushing my hips slowly forward.

She didn't move, nor take off the towel.

You know I'm watching. You know I'm waiting. Is this my payback from the roof?

In that moment, I craved to be between her thighs. I yearned to smell her pussy, wet and in front of me. I wanted to stick my fingers inside of her, pull them out, and lick her juices off.

And all because she stood there in that doorway, hiding that sweet body in shadows.

If you continue with this game, mysh, I'll be bending you over at the nearest surface and fucking you.

My cock twitched in my hand at the thought.

Take off the towel.

I gripped my cock hard as it painfully waited for pleasure, some sort of release.

Unfortunately, she flipped the bathroom light off. Moonlit darkness covered the room.

Ivan, you should have put in night cameras.

I was close to murdering the man. The soft sound of footsteps rose. Then, the teasing noise of material moving. I had no idea, if she was changing or not.

Minutes later, she left her bedroom and went to the living room where Luka sat on the couch. She was fully closed.

I cursed under my breath, *"'tchyo za ga'lima?"*

The rest of the night she sat on her computer and I fell asleep with blue balls for the first time since my teen years.

Now what are you doing, Emily?

Act Two

Definition of Dirty
2: likely to cause disgrace or scandal
dirty little secrets
dirty little lies

Chapter 9
Kazimir

The next morning, I rode in the back of the limo, heading toward Emily's brownstone.

Let's see what she will look like today.

Her strip tease on camera shoved me further into horniness. All night I pictured Emily down on her knees. For some reason, I craved to watch her surrender, to give me pure submission, something she'd probably never given anyone.

Fantasies played out in my head the rest of the night, disturbing my sleep—Emily on her knees, lips parted, taking my cock deep down her throat, begging for more even as she gagged, even as saliva dripped out the corners of her mouth, even as I came all over that beautiful face.

Nasty. Dirty. Filthy thoughts.

They plagued my head. Had me stroking my cock all morning in the shower. Tugging the tip. Thinking of Emily as I got myself off.

By the time, I finally had release there was one dominant thought in my mind.

I won't fuck her. Dangerous. She's too fucking dangerous.

I didn't like the reaction she'd inspired in my body.

And she could hide and change her appearance too fast.

Too tricky.

I'd heard of a woman having many looks, changing their hair and clothes, but Emily had transformed into another person from when I'd met her earlier. And it wasn't just the wig and clothes. On the roof, I felt I'd met bits of the real her. She'd been exposed somehow. Maybe it was the sex. Or it could've been the change of clothes too. She probably used the objects as masks for who she really was.

So many goddamn questions that she's brought up, and none of the answers would deal with my oncoming war.

Emily would just be the washer. An important position, but not enough for me to spend too much time over. Someone was killing my people, and it was all connected, but I didn't know how.

No more letting this one get to my cock. She'll play her position and then I'll move my focus to my enemies.

I arrived at Emily's place.

She was already outside. Luka was on her right. The limo pulled up right in front of her.

I stepped outside.

And we gazed at the other.

Silence stood between us.

Her hair and style were completely different again. A curly afro surrounded her head in a big halo. Tiny candy curls and spirals outlined her face and fell to her shoulders in deep waves. Designer black glasses covered her eyes. Candy red lipstick decorated those delicious lips.

My gaze traveled down her body.

And all my control rushed away. The first time I'd met her, she'd given me a professional feel mixed with artsy creative. The second time, she looked like one of those movie burglaries, creeping into a laser-lined museum to steal a special diamond.

In this moment, she was a femme fatale. I'd already had a hard time not bending her over last night and getting my cock wet. Today would be a battle.

She wore a slim fit checkered dress—black, white, and red. Cinched at the waist. Hugging her curves—full breasts, amazing hips, plump ass. Chic and ultra-designer. As if she stole it off a New York Fashion Week runaway, before the model could go out and show it. Rolex on the wrist. Leather clutch in the other hand. Open-toed midnight black pumps finished the look.

The top of her dress dipped into her full cleavage. It didn't show enough. It was a merciless tease. Just a glimpse. Yesterday, I'd known she had a nice rack. Today, my cock guaranteed it. In my head, I pictured my hands caressing those lush breasts. They were more than a handful. They would overflow and spill out between my fingers.

My cock was harder than it had ever been in my life, and I hadn't even touched her.

Dangerous.

I gripped the door hard and held it open for her. "Good morning, Emily."

With a neutral expression, she gazed at me through those dark glasses. "Good morning, Kazimir."

My name sounded like salted caramel on her tongue, and no matter how I tried to push the vision away, in that moment, I imagined her licking my balls as she whispered it. And also moaning my name as I pounded into her. Those perfectly painted candy red lips would be smeared from so much licking and sucking and groaning.

This is why she's so dangerous.

The thought of her sucking me off had me tenting the front of my slacks. Annoyed that her simple words had caused the reaction, I didn't hide my hardening cock.

Let her see what she does to me. It doesn't matter. I'm still the one in control.

Silent, we stood in front of the other, almost trying to exert our dominance.

Instead of climbing into the limo, her naughty eyes roamed down my suit to where my arousal displayed for all to see.

You see what you're doing to me?

Her breath hitched. Inch by inch, she guided her gaze back to mine. Silence sat between us. What could I say to her in that moment, but that I didn't want her to climb into the limo anymore. Instead I wanted her to climb onto my cock and bounce that sweet fat ass up and down on it.

With her lips parted, she stared at me. Did she think she was say, watching me through those sunglasses? Did she feel the intense sexual pull between us?

I licked my lips, and her gaze goes to my mouth, studying my tongue. I need her to see my tongue and think about it between her thighs, lapping at that wet pussy. I want her moistness on my tongue.

My voice came out as a growl. "What's on your mind, *mysh*?"

She widened her eyes and then got into the limo.

I smiled.

My little mysh is always full of surprises.

I climbed in after her. My cock weighed heavy in my pants.

We sped off minutes later.

Smart, she didn't ask where we were going, just gazed out of the window as if assessing for herself where we were heading.

"How long have you lived in Harlem?" I asked.

She continued to stare out of the window, her face hidden from me. "Born and raised."

"Have you ever wanted to go somewhere else?"

"Yes."

"Where?"

"Anywhere."

You're answering my questions, but not truly answering them. You're so careful and always in control.

I'd checked her video footage from last night. She hadn't even gone to bed. Luka had sat on her living room couch. She'd been propped in a big recliner chair, under a blanket, binge-watching movies all night, while she typed into her laptop. My tech guy had said that she'd been doing research online the whole time—not an email or any of her social media. For those hours she'd been researching skyscrapers for sale in Manhattan—doing her job, before I'd asked.

"Did you sleep well?" I asked, wondering how truthful she would be with me.

"No, but I didn't try to sleep." She turned away from the window, opened her clutch, and pulled out two folded pieces of paper. "I found two buildings you might be interested in. The one on Madison Avenue is my favorite. It's 1.2 million-square-foot property. Valued at 2.25 billion."

"I thought you weren't comfortable with washing millions, now you would consider billions?"

She looked at me. "I'm thinking that once you've signed over Rumi's money to me—"

"How did you know that was what we would be doing today?"

"It would be the smartest move," she said. "And I believe you are a smart man."

"Who told you Rumi died?"

"Everyone in Harlem knew by the end of my art showing last night."

"That's not an answer, Emily."

"A friend told me."

"And you put two and two together about why I needed you?"

"Yes."

"And your thoughts on Rumi?" I asked.

"The cops say it was a suicide."

For some reason, I told her. "He was murdered."

"I figured. But either way, if you're able to get cops to lie about the cause of death, then you would be able to get lawyers and judges to approve a fake will, naming me as the head beneficiary for all of his millions...which are really all of your millions."

I drank in those sexy legs, unable to help myself. Nothing made me crazier than a gorgeous woman that could outwit me.

"So. . ." Catching me look at her legs, she blushed.

"Go ahead, little *mysh*. You were impressing me."

"Mysh?"

"Mouse in Russian."

A smile broke across her face, before she shook it away.

"You find the nickname humorous?"

"Yes. My favorite English teacher used to call me Mouse. She would say, 'that girl is as sneaky and crafty like a mouse. Watch out for her. She disappears through the walls, and you can't find the damn girl until the food comes out for lunch.'" And then she stopped herself as if she hadn't wanted to give me too much information about her.

"Anyway." She sighed. "With my new inheritance from Rumi, I would have enough capital to make a bank interested enough with loaning the money to purchase the building on Madison Ave."

"We won't have to try too hard to get a bank interested. Many will do business with me. They just want a squeaky-clean name on the documents."

"Mine?"

"Yes."

She let out a long breath. "So...about my name being on the documents."

"You're my washer."

"Yes." She tapped her fingers on her thigh. "I was just wondering how long I would be your washer."

"You think this is just a temporary deal?"

"I was thinking I could wash for you until you've dealt with this Rumi situation and found a new person. Of course, my brother would be released safely to me by then."

I smirked. "Of course."

She took off her sunglasses and hit me with those dazzling brown eyes that made me think of chocolate on my tongue.

"Could we work out a temporary arrangement?" she asked. "Six months. A year."

"You don't like the idea of being in bed with me forever?"

At the mention of the word *bed*, she blinked, but grabbed control of her reaction. "I don't like to be in bed with anyone forever."

Interesting.

I raised my eyebrows. "No dreams of marriage and kids?"

"I. . .I thought we were talking about business."

"We are. I'm just wondering."

"Correct. No dreams of marriage and kids. And no dreams of a full-time. . .employer either."

"Have I offended you?" I asked.

"No."

"Do I smell? Am I unpleasing to look at?"

Her breath hitched in her throat as she cleared her throat and answered, "No. You smell. . .good, and you're handsome."

My entire life, women told me I was handsome. But women tended to say those things when one was the most powerful man in the room. Never did I truly believe their compliments.

Yet, hearing Emily say it made me feel different.

"You like to be the boss of yourself?"

"Yes." She nodded as if excited that I understood.

I reached out my hand and touched one of the thousands of little spiral curls. I couldn't help myself. I'd been wanting to run my fingers through them since I'd first spotted her.

Is this another disguise, mysh?

Against all sanity, I pulled a curl close to me, wanting to reveal what she was hiding underneath the wig.

Her head went with my hand. "Ouch."

I let go. "Sorry."

"What. . .?" She opened her mouth, gave me a crazy look, and then laughed. "No disrespect, but what were you doing?"

I pointed at her hair. "This isn't a wig?"

"No." Her cheeks rose with humor as if she was keeping more laughter back and doing a bad job of it. "This is my hair."

"You took it out of the braids?"

"Yes."

"But that was a lot of work."

"It doesn't matter. My hook-up braids fast."

"So, she'll do another design again?"

"Maybe." She quirked her eyebrows. "Do you really like hair?"

"No. I really like uniqueness. It always traps my attention, and so far, you've intrigued me."

Her smile fell away. She was smart enough to know that my attention would not be one of a regular man. Men like me collected things that we liked. We held onto them, never letting go, never giving them their freedom.

"So, that is why you didn't sleep last night? You stayed up doing research, thinking this through and trying to find the best way to get rid of me, without pissing me off," I said. "You wanted to wash a huge amount of money for me fast. You figured billions would do the job. How could I say no? And then I would give you Darryl and set you free, having another washer to simply watch the building."

She put those glasses back on, turned away, and stared out of the window. "And your thoughts on my plan? Was it foolish or am I getting warm?"

"Yes. You're getting very warm, *mysh*. So close, it'll be hot soon. But it's not going in the direction you're hoping for."

She continued to gaze out the window, never giving me a reaction.

She's back to hiding. At least, I've got to see a little of her today.

The limo stopped in front of a five-level building right at the center of the Financial District. It was a neighborhood located at the southern tip of Manhattan stacked with corporate offices and the headquarters of many major financial institutions. But the district's namedroppers were the New York Stock Exchange, the Federal Reserve, and Wall Street. It was where Rumi's lawyer's office was located.

Emily had been right. We were going to sign over his money to her and begin the process of her washing my money.

We sat there in silence.

I wouldn't let us leave, until she'd said something. I had to know her level of commitment. It didn't matter, if she wanted to work with me or not. What mattered was if she was so desperate to be free of my hold that she tried to escape—or even worse—went to authorities.

After a few minutes, she turned my way and broke the silence. "I understand your position. I'm wondering, if you would be open to a compromise in the future. . .when things are less stressful."

"Compromise?"

"There could be something that I could do for you that could be more valuable than my washing."

"Something to give you your freedom?"

"Yes."

"Interesting." I loved her line of thinking, but doubted she was envisioning what I was. "What comes to your mind now?"

"I will wash as much money as you need—"

"You'll do that regardless. I want a kiss."

She opened her mouth in shock. "A kiss?"

"Yes."

"You're. . .you're playing around."

"I am, but you must agree that a kiss would help your negotiation."

"I. . .I don't kiss. . .the people I work for."

"I've heard about the people you work for. That's a smart rule."

Luka opened her side of the door.

She stepped out, probably nervous I was going to kiss her. I'd been thinking about it. I climbed out after her. Luka waited on her side.

I touched her arm, before she could walk toward the building.

She faced me.

"You brought up some good points," I said. "And you've impressed me with your research on the building purchases last night."

"Thank you."

"I'll think about what you said in the limo."

She sighed. "Thank you."

I gestured to Luka. "Let's go."

And then she turned around, studied the building, and didn't move. "No."

Through her sunglasses, I caught her eyes darting from side to side as if counting something or someone. "Umm. . .we should really get back in the limo—"

"Why?" I asked.

"Too many Jamaicans." She backed away with a big smile and opened the door. "I'll explain. . .and if you could not make a big thing about it. . .that would be really good. . ."

Luka scowled, still pissed with her from disappearing last night. "You don't give out orders, only—"

"No," I said in Russian. I didn't even look across the street, following what she'd said. "Let's get in the limo, but like Emily said, don't make it a big deal."

Luka grumbled, but walked forward.

I let her get in first and climbed in afterwards.

She blew out a long breath. "Can he park the limo in the parking lot, so it won't spook them? They'll think we're still going in."

"The Jamaicans?"

"Yes."

I turned on my phone, called my driver, and gave him the orders.

He started the limo and slowly drove us toward the back of the building. But as we journeyed there, I spotted what Emily did. There were twenty men sporadically scattered around the block. All had dreadlocks and wore gray or black suits. Most had them in pulled back and placed in ponytails.

"So, this is a Jamaican gang?" I asked.

"Yeah. *Shower Posse*. Others say Jamaican posse. It's a loose coalition of gangs, based predominantly in Kingston, London, New York City, and Toronto." Still studying the figures outside, she took off her shades and put them in her clutch. "Drugs and arms trafficking. They're big, but not on your level so they've probably never crossed your radar."

"And why should I be worried about them today?"

"New York is cliquish with their crime. Very exclusive. Everyone stays in their place." She looked over her shoulder at the cars parking behind us in the lot. Some were my men. Others were ones I didn't recognize. "Shower Posse rocks hard in Harlem and Brooklyn. Their lawyer is in Chinatown. Their washer is in Little Italy. There's no reason for them to be here in the financial district. It's too many of them."

"They've come here to fight or kill."

"Exactly...and..."She leaned forward and gazed out of my window, counting under her breath. "Shit...fuck."

"What do you see?"

"At least sixty fucking people with guns that aren't Russian. They must be Shower Posse. Unless there's some sort of Rasta Gun Business conference I don't know about."

I scanned the space. There were men in suits standing in front of the bank and they looked like they had guns. There was no doubt about that. I checked at the store across from the bank. Four other Jamaicans in suits stupidly held newspapers up in front of them as if they'd all come to that location to meet and read the paper.

"I've only counted ten men," I said.

"The vans."

Pissed, I checked behind the limo and spotted six different vans parked in various parts of the lot. In all of them, a man with dreadlocks sat at the wheel. I was sure there were a bunch of men in each van.

Emily's right. It's probably sixty.

I frowned. "Good count."

She leaned back in the chair. "There's some guys on the roof of the restaurant across the street too. They aren't snipers or anything. Too stupid to not let me see them."

I grinned.

She raised her eyebrows. "What's so funny?"

"You're good."

"Someone's trying to kill you or me. . .or us both."

"This isn't a new thing for me." I shrugged. "And recently, someone has been murdering my employees."

"So, I picked a hell of a time to start working for you then."

"You did. Last night, I found one of my madams dead."

"The madam at that place I met you at last night?"

"Yes."

"She knew something?" Emily asked.

"She did."

"And the Shower Posse knows something too."

"Yes. They know who's trying to kill me, because what else could this be?" I asked.

"This is weird." Emily shook her head. "It seems like this was all planned, but how would anyone know that you'd be in New York? Are you usually here?"

"No, but the men close to me would've known that I would come to New York, if my washer was killed."

"So, whoever killed your washer is trying to get rid of you?"

"Yes."

"And they're close to you."

I clenched my jaw. "I hope not for their sake."

She blew out an exasperated breath. "Are we going to leave?"

"No." I gestured at the parking lot's exit where a van had coincidentally blocked the area as soon as we'd stopped. "They plan on keeping us in this parking lot."

"But they haven't attacked yet." She tapped her thigh. "That means something."

"It does. They may just want us to go in the building."

She never stopped tapping that finger. "Or to shoot us as we get out."

"No. They see my men." I gestured at them. "It would be a fifty-fifty chance on who would survive."

My guys had parked too. They were good enough to have probably noticed the presence of armed men in the area and were waiting for my command.

"Who knew you were coming here?" she asked.

I thought of the small list. Not many knew. Even my driver hadn't given the instructions until ten minutes before the time. If he was giving out the information, we would've beat the Jamaicans here.

I studied some of them. Boredom decorated their face. Every now and then they glanced at the limo but hadn't touched their guns or even made a move.

"I'm supposed to go inside the building. They're not here for me."

Emily nodded. "They're here to kill your men."

"And whoever is in the building, or on the floor with the lawyer, that's who's supposed to kill me."

She pulled her phone out of the clutch, turned it on, and wrote in it.

"What are you doing?" I asked.

"Looking up the building's floor plan."

"Interesting." I should've been worried, but I'd maneuvered out of scarier situations than this.

I was more worried about keeping her safe, she was not only my washer, but becoming an important asset to have on my team. Her speedy alertness had noticed that the Jamaicans were out of place and from that she'd logically concluded to at least get me back in the limo to assess the situation further.

I'm sorry, mysh, but how can I ever let go of you now?

"Okay." She shut the phone off and faced me. "I've got an idea. Do you trust me?"

"For now."

"Here's what we should do."

Chapter 10
Emily

We left the limo. My bodyguard Luka stayed on my right. Kazimir walked on my left. No one was on his side. My nerves flared. Logically, I would want my new employer to remain alive. If someone was killing his people, and trying to murder him and me today, I most certainly wanted him to be victorious.

"I really think someone should be with you too," I whispered as we crossed the street.

"No." Kazimir unbuttoned his jacket. "Then, it will look like I noticed something was wrong. I usually keep my guards several feet around me, but not too close that it's suffocating. We should continue to look the part."

Dread hit me, but I stayed the course. Kazimir had two guns with him, one in each holster under his jacket. Confidence glittered in his eyes. I had no doubt that he knew how to use them.

"You just stay alive." Kazimir placed his hand at the corner of my back, and the spot warmed from his fingers. "And stay close to me."

"I will." Inching to him as we hit the pavement, so that we appeared more as lovers taking a stroll.

He slipped his hand to my hip and tightened the grip. "When we're safe, I'll make sure that your bother comes home tonight. I owe you for right now."

Surprised, I almost stumbled, but kept my balance and continued to follow Luka who marched in front of us, studying each suited Shower Posse member in front of the building.

"Stay calm, Luka," Kazimir said, "We don't shoot unless we have to. Save your bullets for inside."

The bulky man said nothing.

We arrived at the building.

I didn't make a big show of it, but I studied some of the Jamaican gang members closer. They never reached for their guns the closer they got, still staring at the cars full of Kazimir's men.

Kazimir had been right. The guys standing outside was to make sure Kazimir didn't have back up, when he needed help from whatever was going to happen inside.

Kazimir brushed his lips against my ear. "Giggle as if I've said something funny and you love me."

I giggled and tenderly hit his chest. "Oh, stop it, Kaz. You're such a bad boy."

"Oh, Emily. You haven't seen bad yet." Playfully growling, he moved his hand to my ass and squeezed it hard.

I gasped, "Kaz."

He laughed, yet desire blazed in his gaze.

Luka opened the door for us as he scanned the front. There was a hall. Ten feet down was a metal detector with two men dressed in cop uniforms. One had a scruffy beard and dreads hanging from his cap which I didn't think cops even wore inside buildings.

I whispered, "Definitely not cops."

"Luka, kill them."

Luka grunted.

We stopped in front.

One of them stepped up. "Do you have any—"

In a flash, Luka pointed the gun at his head and pulled the trigger. The bullet hit the center of his eyes. Before the man dropped to the floor, Luka shot the other. Again, right between the eyes—no hesitation. Minimal blood. Just a dripping from the bullet lodged in their skulls.

Damn.

We walked through the metal detectors. Bells ringed as we passed. It didn't matter. No one was in the lobby anyway. Someone had cleared the building.

I glanced behind my shoulder.

No one had come behind us.

"What do you think?" Kazimir asked me.

Luka scowled. "We're following *her*?"

"She's the one that noticed the Jamaicans here in the first place."

Luka gave no retort.

I checked the elevators and spotted the fire exit I'd seen in the building's lay out on my phone. "We can't go upstairs. It could be something like a bomb or—"

Luka snorted.

I raised my hands in the air. "Hey, I know it sounds crazy, but I'm not going upstairs. They cleared the building. Why? Due to a possible gun battle? I doubt it."

"So, we go out the back?" Luka gestured with his gun. "Guys will be there."

"No." I shook my head. "That's not the plan."

Kazimir smiled. "Apparently, Ms. Chambers can get us out of the building without no one seeing us."

Luka rolled his eyes. "What are we doing? This is too dangerous. I should have not let you come in here, sir."

"I can get us out of here." I looked up at the ceiling. "We just have to hurry."

"Because of a bomb?" Luka snorted.

"Yes." I kicked off my shoes, picked them up, and scurried away. I would've been able to run, but the dress was too tight. Had I been truly thinking, I would've worn pants.

But Kazimir had made me wet last night, and I wanted to get him back. His erection when I walked up to the limo, was well worth my hurt feet.

He started it.

But now, I would be ruining the shoes and the dress. Because where I had to take them, nothing would get the stench off us.

They followed my fast walk to the fire exit.

"There will be men behind the building," Luka grumbled.

"We're not leaving the building." I went to the door on the right of the fire exit and turned the knob. It was locked. Luka was too busy to notice, as he gazed out of the fire exit's tiny window glass.

Kazimir took one of the guns hidden under his jacket. "Stand back."

He shot the knob. The door swung open on its own from the impact, revealing a rusty dark room that led off to somewhere that wasn't used.

"They're fighting outside." Luka gripped his gun with both hands. "Wherever she's taking us, we need to go now."

"Come on." I turned on my phone and shined the light inside. "We'll have to go in there. It will lead us to Farley-Morgan tunnel right under 9th avenue."

"In here." Luka pointed with his gun. "This is your way out."

Kazimir curved his full lips into a smile. "Genius. That's how you escaped Luka last night."

I slung my shoes inside the dark space. I wouldn't take the heels with me now, but maybe I could come back and get them.

We headed inside. The door slammed behind us. I shined the light along the room. Cigarette butts and dirt covered the floor. I hated not having my shoes on.

"Some of the janitors or maintenance probably smoke in here, during the winter, when they don't want to go outside." I stepped forward.

Kazimir stopped me. "No."

"What?"

He put his gun up and then picked me up as I protested, "What are you—"

"No. You don't have any shoes on."

I struggled to get out of his arms. "I can't walk in this tunnel with those heels on."

He gripped me hard and walked forward. "I'll carry you, until you can walk in those heels. Luka, grab them."

The big man did it.

I tried to get free. "Kazimir, it's a long fucking hike—"

"And you are the small woman who saved my life." He smiled within my cellphone's light.

"I haven't saved it yet—"

An explosion stopped my sentence. It came from up above, rocking the entire foundation. We all fell to the ground, yet somehow Kazimir had kept his hold on me, so that when we fell, he hit the concrete first.

My phone cracked somewhere next to me. It was complete dark. And then a boom vibrated through the concrete just like an earthquake must've felt like. Sirens blared off in the distance, but I couldn't hear them that well. Everything was muffled. More cracks and noises rose.

Still, Kazimir held me as all three of us listened to the horror above.

"Are you okay?" Kazimir whispered in my ear.

I couldn't see him, but clung to his hard body, knowing I would be okay as long as he was near. "Yes. I'm fine. But my phone is probably broken."

Luka sounding more chipper, volunteered, "She can use my phone, if she needs to."

I reached out and then I paused. "Maybe, we shouldn't turn on your phones. Someone could track them and know that you both are still alive."

"And I would like them to think we're dead." Kazimir helped me up in the darkness.

I inched close to him, smoothing my body against his and not caring how he took it. This was a time for survival, not for manners and insecurities.

"Do you think you can find her phone on the ground, Luka?" Kazimir asked.

Scuffling sounded near my right. Another explosion crashed through the short silence. I didn't know if the person had put a bunch of bombs up on Rumi's lawyer's floor or if the bomb had triggered other things to explode.

"I've got it." Luka must've pressed for it to come on because a light streamed from his hand, and partly illuminated the room. He handed it to me. Luka's words swam in a thicker accent than Kazimir. "Good call on the tunnel."

"Thanks, I'm big on staying alive." I took the phone.

Kazimir picked me up.

I protested again, "I don't think—"

"I thought the bomb ended that argument." Kazimir carried me forward. "Which way do we go?"

"We keep walking until we see red smiley faces."

"Why smiley faces?" Kazimir asked.

"That's how Max, Theo, and I would find out way around the tunnels. We would draw them all over the walls and floor with hidden arrows to show us how to get out."

"Hmmm." His chest tensed against me. "Whose idea was the smiley faces?"

"Always Max. Why?"

"I'm just wondering about meaningful coincidences."

Chapter 11
Emily

We continued down the hallway. A moldy scent filled the air. Large cob webs dangled in corners. Rats scurried by. Luka jumped and came close to shooting one.

"Save your bullets, Luka," Kazimir said.

"I hate rats," the man grumbled as he stomped forward.

"How long have you all been marking these tunnels?" Kazimir asked.

"Since we were kids."

"Who else knows about them?"

"I'm sure the city and retired maintenance and train workers. People like that, but it's not something that others know." Enjoying Kazimir carrying me quite too much, I shined the cellphone along the walls. The man was a muscled personification of contradictions. His arms were hard, yet soft. So close, he smelled dangerous, but I absolutely felt safe.

"So, only your brother and this Maxwell knows about these tunnels?" Kazimir asked.

"My friend Kennedy too, but she almost never goes down with us, so she wouldn't know her way. It's always been a big secret of mine." I considered what I'd said and almost cursed at myself.

I'd just led Kazimir and Luka into my biggest escape method. Now if I ever had to get away from the Russians I would need another way. Fear knotted at the pit of my stomach.

Let's hope I don't have a reason to escape.

We must've walked for twenty minutes in dark silence with only the cellphone's light guiding the way.

I wondered what both men were thinking.

Surely, they'd dealt with worse in Russia. Their lives couldn't have been perfect white picket fenced houses full of love. These guys were big, tattooed, and rough. That came from hard living and a tough life.

Kazimir held me the whole time, never stopping to rest his arms. The butt of one gun tapped against my side every other step.

But I had no reason to complain. His arms were safe and comfortable. Warm and powerful. His scent drew me closer. For those minutes of silence, I'd been wondering what his cologne was mixed with—pine or maybe a designer musk. Something expensive and exclusive. Other minutes of silence I yearned to lean my had against his shoulder and rub my face against his chin and neck.

So close, I'd been imagining licking and kissing it. Doing dirty, nasty things to it.

"What's on your mind, my little *mysh*?" Kazimir whispered through the silence.

I licked my lips. "I'm just thinking."

"About?"

How sexy and strong you are.

"This whole thing must've been planned a long time ago," I said instead. "The bomb. Rumi's death. It's all very well calculated. Killing Rumi would've been hard. Personally, I thought I would be the only person that could do it."

"Why?"

"I. . .uh. . .just thought so," I muttered, realizing that my true response might not have showed me in the best light.

"What were you going to say?" Kazimir pushed further. "We're friends now. We know each other's secrets."

"Do we?" I enjoyed the comfort of his arms to much no matter how I tried not to. I cleared my throat. "You know about my tunnels. What secret do I know of yours?"

"That someone close to me is trying to kill me. That would be valuable information to any of my enemies. What else do you want to know, Emily?"

"Where's my brother?"

"At the brothel you were at last night."

"How long has he been there?"

"Since you said you would work for me."

"He's safe?" I asked.

"Of course."

"And you'll bring him to me tonight?"

"Yes."

"Okay." I sighed. "I was going to say that I'm the only one that has a secret passageway into Rumi's building. It was why I set him up in that building years ago."

Kazimir stopped and turned to me. "Secret passage?"

"Yes. The stairwell doesn't stop on the second floor. You can keep going down to the basement. And there's a door for an old boiler room that they don't use anymore when they renovated the place."

"And the boiler room leads you to a tunnel?"

"An old subway track to be exact, which could link you up to anywhere."

"So, whoever killed Rumi probably knew about that passageway?"

"No."

He started walking. "Why do you say no?"

"Because that would mean that either Darryl, Maxwell, or I killed him. And that's not the case. Darryl couldn't kill anyone. Maybe get someone to do it, but he wouldn't be able to do it himself. Maxwell would only do it if. . ."

"What?"

I'm telling him too fucking much.

I gritted my teeth. "Maxwell would do it, if I asked."

"He loves you?"

"Like a brother."

"Hmmm. And what about you? Where were you when Rumi was killed?"

"I was busy. . .dating." At least I think so. I was damn sure too fucked up to kill someone. "Anyway, I don't think anyone would've used the passageway."

"Maybe, we could check it out and see later."

"Maybe." And then excitement rushed through my veins. "There's a smiley face."

Several little red ones covered the wall and then ran into a line continuing before us.

Luka and Kazimir saw the smiley faces and then exchanged looks.

I shifted in his arms. "Do you need to rest?"

"No. I'm ready to get above ground."

"Okay. We're close to my gallery."

There's no way I'm showing you the tunnels that lead back to my house.

Another twenty minutes passed. We made it to the ladder that lead up to my office's closet. Kazimir let me down. Luka handed me my shoes.

"Thanks."

Kazimir studied the ladder and then the tunnel. "I can't believe you walked down here last night. Were you by yourself?"

"Yes." Holding my shoes and phone, I managed to climb up the ladder, but very slowly. "I do it all the time."

"Not anymore."

"It's safe," I said.

"I'm putting more men on you."

"I know how to keep myself safer than any of your men could—"

"The discussion is over."

Oh, really?! The discussion is not over. I am having it in my head! And I say I'm going back into the tunnels again. So, there!

Frowning, I made it to the top of the ladder, opened the hatch, and scooted out.

Luka came up after me and immediately checked my office. "No one's in here. I'll check out in the gallery and the outside. Stay inside the office until I get back."

"Okay." I nodded.

Kazimir appeared next and then shut the hatch. "I can't believe you walk down there by yourself."

I placed my hands on my hips. "No one's ever attacked me."

He squared off on me as if asserting his authority over me. "Because even crazy people have their limits, and even a serial killer would think twice about going down there."

I smirked as I looked up at him. "My tunnels scare you?"

"No." He brushed off the dust on his arm. "But, your tunnels showed you in another light. You intrigue and scare me."

I backed away from him. "How so?"

"It showed me that you're not scared of a lot." He took off his jacket and placed it on my desk. His muscles rippled under the crisp material. "A person that can walk in darkness for close to an hour by themselves, in some tunnel under a city where no one could hear you scream. . .that is a person that I wouldn't want to go up against."

"I'll take that as a compliment."

"You should." He raised his eyebrows. "How can you stay down there by yourself for so long?"

The question made me uncomfortable. "It's not a big deal."

"It is. How long have you been hiding in the dark?"

All my life.

I crossed my arms across my chest. "Some little girls have to hide more than others."

An intensity blazed in his eyes. "You're quite a woman. You saved me twice. First from the Jamaicans, and then from the bomb. What do you want?"

"I get something?"

"Yes."

"Two things. You'll already get your brother back, so pick two other favors."

I turned around and headed to my coffee machine on the other side of the room, needing something to do with my hands. First, I was too eager to ask him for the only thing I wanted—freedom. I had to play it right or lose. He'd already promised to hand over Darryl. I should just focus on the freedom.

But then the second reason I'd gone to the coffee maker was because without that jacket he looked damn good. And I'd been full anxiety after the bomb. What I needed right now was a good fuck on the desk to straighten my nerves out.

But Kazimir wouldn't be a smart choice. He was too dangerous, and now he knew too much about me. He knew my escape routes, and although it would still take them time to find me if I hid down in the tunnels, they could find me.

I didn't like that at all.

If I fucked a guy, I barely wanted him to know my real name. The less information, the less they came back.

No. I can't fuck him. Somehow, he's gotten too close.

"Would you like some coffee, while Luka clears my gallery?" I glanced over my shoulder. "I can get a pot brewing."

"No, thank you. Your tunnels walk was enough stimulation for today."

Our gazes met.

I grinned.

Kazimir leaned against my desk with those sexy, bulging arms. His shirt stretched around those muscles. It didn't even feel like my office anymore with him in it. He suddenly owned every inch of the space. And he watched me with intensity.

Warmth pooled between my thighs. His gaze penetrated. It was heat and desire. Physical and intimate. A vision flashed through my head—him and I writhing together in the darkness of my bedroom.

It would be so good. His gaze had promised that. I could see it in those thick lashes and sexy eyes.

"You were dating the night Rumi died?" he asked.

I blinked caught off guard. "Something like that."

"Who were you dating?"

"No one in particular."

"Explain."

"They're not dates. They're hook ups. Just a little...something...to keep the edge off."

He licked his lips in response.

I swore heat reached out from his eyes, threatening to burn me. Instantly, I thought about how he could take care of me. One of his favors could be his cock. Surely, he would not only keep the edge off, my body would probably crumble under his frame.

It would be so damn good.

"I just met the guy and had a fling."

"You're very truthful."

When I want to be.

"Where did you meet this person?" he asked.

"From the Tinder app on my phone."

Kazimir frowned, but that erotic warmth in his eyes never left. "Do you always do that?"

"Yes." I averted his heated gaze.

"But, what about the Tinder Killer?"

"He's killing men."

"You should still be careful."

"If you don't mind me asking...why are *you* asking about this? Why does my sex life matter?"

"I wondered what type of man would get your attention."

"I guess it would be one that likes abandoned subway tunnels."

That expression of lust didn't change on his face.

In my mind, I could feel his hard muscles beneath my fingertips, his firm body moving over me, his thick, fat cock filling and stretching me.

I stirred in place, pushing the image away.

The room went warm. So much that I would've been happy, if we both took off our clothes.

Fuck. I need to masturbate or something. This is insane.

I cleared my throat. "And what do you do? I doubt you go on Tinder."

"I have a few women who I call to please me."

"You sound like a king."

He didn't respond as he continued to trap me in that intense gaze.

"Well. . ." I shifted my weight to my other feet not used to being off balance like this. "It must be good to have someone that's *on call* to please you."

"And you have difficulty with that, Emily?"

"Yes. At the present moment, my new employer told me that I'm not allowed to date."

"He sounds mean."

"Bosses are bosses. Either way, I won't be able to. . .you know?" I shrugged. "I won't be able to get the edge off."

"Correct." He growled the word. "You'll be busy."

"Yes." I bit my bottom lip, unable to look away from him. "I'll be busy."

Okay. New topic.

In a low tone, he whispered, "Come here."

An instant blast of heat flooded me. My breath caught in my throat. I knew what those words really meant. They were lathered in lust. Dotted in hunger. And sex was all over his face, thickening in the air. I could taste it on my tongue, and I loved the sweetness.

That accent made his voice even more delicious as he licked his lips. "Emily."

Slowly, I walked over to him.

I'm not going to have sex with him. I'm not going to have sex with him.

I stopped right in front of him. An inch closer and my breasts would've touched his chest.

He raised his hand to my head and ran his fingers through my curls. "This is how I like your hair."

I blushed.

"I'm just telling you, but I know you will look different tomorrow and the day after that and the day after." He slipped his hand to the back of my head and fisted my curls into his hand. No pain came, but he had a strong hold on me. "Beautiful. Stunning. But then, you're more than that."

I didn't whimper or gasp, although I wanted to. But for some reason, I had to show that I was tough. I had to prove that he wasn't getting to me, even though every inch of my body screamed for him to fuck me.

He tossed me a wicked smile. "I'm sure I'll like all of the other looks too. I love your surprises."

I just gazed at him, so lost in his heat—the way he could dominate me with ease and come closer to me than any other had ever come.

"What you did earlier today, not many would've done the same, especially in your position. You saved Luka and my life." Still fisting my hair, he gently leaned my head back, exposing the curve of my neck to him. "So, I will give you two favors. But there's one wish that I won't ever give you."

My chest rose and fell. He pressed against me so close that when my breasts rose with my breathing, my nipples rubbed against his muscular chest.

"For now, I don't know if I can give you a temporary employment deal." He slipped his lips along the curve of my neck. "You're too smart. Too valuable. And too goddamn sexy. I like seeing you. Smelling you. I want to touch your skin too much."

A whimper escaped me.

"I don't like the idea of temporary, when it comes to you, Emily." He nibbled at the curve, driving me crazy. My knees almost gave way. I leaned into him more as I arched my back, wanting to feel more of him. A thrill moved through me. Exciting. Intoxicating.

"And on the topic of your dating, I don't want anyone else. . .keeping the edge off." He growled those last words as he slipped his lips along my chin and then stopped at my mouth.

I shuddered against him, but still he didn't kiss me.

I almost begged him too.

"Don't be mad at me, little *mysh*."

"I'm not," I whispered.

"Hmmm." And then his mouth went to mine before I could process what was happening. I thought a kiss from him would be rough and fast with the way, but it's sweet, warm, and so soft. He took his time, giving me lazy wet strokes of his tongue, savoring my taste.

"Oh, *mysh*." He captured my lips again, sweeping his tongue over mine and then fully claiming my mouth for his. Consuming me. His scent filled the air to the point where I knew I would smell like him the rest of the night—powerful and seductively masculine.

"You've taken good care of me today," he whispered against my lips. "Besides giving you those two favors, you should let me further take care of you."

Before I could respond, he stole another kiss.

Fuck!

And when he nibbled my bottom lip, desire shot through me. I needed more too. Whimpering, I rose on my tippy toes and wrapped my arms around his shoulders, needing to taste more of him. I sucked on his tongue, and he groaned in pure male pleasure, triggering carnal need to slice up my body.

And for several hot minutes, we finished the conversation without words. It was gasps and throaty moans. Lips smacking and sensual grasps of clothing and hair.

As if deranged with lust, he guided me backwards and pushed me up against the wall, cradling my face. Tasting me deeper than any man had ever tried.

My nipples pebbled in my bra. He sucked on my tongue and I could take no more. I didn't even want to come up for air.

I need this.

I raised one of my thighs to his hip, wanting to climb this sexy man and rub my pussy all over him.

"Oh, Emily." Understanding my hunger, he gripped both of my thighs, lifting me up with his palms. I moaned and wrapped my legs around his waist and locked my ankles. I straddled that huge waist. My dress climbed up and gathered above my hips.

He gripped my ass hard—pushing me back and forth between pain and pleasure. And then he ground his hard cock between my thighs, rubbing that thick length against me.

He broke our kiss for an instant, looking into my eyes as he ground into me with slow, meaningful thrusts. Fucking me with clothes on—right through my thin panties. I grew so wet, my pussy probably would stain the front of his pants, but he didn't appear to care as he returned to fucking my mouth with his tongue and continuing to rub his cock rhythmically against my clit.

Someone knocked at the door.

It was most likely Luka.

No. Not right now. Wait.

A dark growl left Kazimir. "What?"

The door opened right as Kazimir gently put me down.

Really, Luka?! I was just starting to like you.

Yanking my dress past my hips, I tried to walk around Kazimir, but he gripped my waist and kept me there.

"No." He kissed me again.

A throat cleared behind us. Luka's rough voice sounded next. "Kazimir, we have a problem."

Groaning, Kazimir dragged his lips from mine. "More problems?"

I took that moment to catch my breath and process Luka's words. But I didn't get the time.

The burly man stepped inside my office.

"There's a dead woman in the back of the gallery," Luka said. "Still warm. We might've just missed who killed her as we were climbing up the ladder. It's our style. Classic. Straight shot to the center of her forehead. No gun or nothing else was left behind."

A dead woman? Who? Why?

Chapter 12
Maxwell

I watched the news. My eyes watered.

"As the death toll continues to rise in the bombing of the Financial District," the news reporter stood in front of the bombed building and spoke into the microphone, *"Authorities believe the man in the street cam's photo is Kazimir Solonik, head of the Russian Mafia known as the Bratva."*

I turned the volume up.

"Solonik is tied to a numerous amount of crimes and has proven ties with terrorists and a direct line to Russian President Vladimir Putin."

Another image flashed of a big bear of a man with scars on his chin.

"Authorities say that the other man in the photo is suspected to be Luka Ivankov also known as The Butcher. He is an infamous hitman whose committed several high-profile murders."

A distorted image of a woman showed on the next screen.

I knew it was Emily.

"Authorities are requesting that anyone call, if they have information about this unidentified woman. The police are slowly trying to piece this situation together and would like anyone to call, no matter how small they think the detail could be."

The screen shifted to the news people back at the station.

"This entire situation is mind-blowing." The male broadcaster had a bad haircut and an ugly suit. *"Now, Patty, do they think these three people were involved in the bombing or the chaotic shooting that happened outside?"*

Patty touched her ear as if just hearing the question, nodded, and spoke, *"Unfortunately, Tim, I believe that these people may be along with the many bodies found in the rubble. Police are just trying to discover why these three individuals were in this location, before the bombing and gunfight ensued. So far. . ."*

I put the television on mute.

She can't be dead. Not Emily.

I gripped the phone in my hand.

Emily had still not answered or texted me back that she was okay.

The news played the bombing all day. I wouldn't have even thought Emily could've been in the facility, until they flashed the Russian mafia boss's face. His photo had been flashing all day. Street cameras had picked up an image of Emily, another big guy, and him walking into the building. Minutes later, it exploded on the third level, dragging down bricks, people, and dust to swarm throughout the Financial District. Traffic had been backed up. Fire trucks and police cars blocked off most of the traffic ways.

News feeds showed dead bodies on the ground.

Jamaicans and Russians? What the fuck is going on today?

I typed into my phone again, knowing it was stupid to do so. Emily hadn't made it. She was dead. Her photo had flashed on the screen next to the Russian. They'd only had the shot from the street camera, unsure of who she was.

The Feds had already done a press conference with the Mayor declaring this a bittersweet victory in the war on organized crime.

She can't be dead. Jamaicans were there, Emily. How did you not think something was up?

Sitting the phone on my coffee table, I rose from the couch and paced in front of the tv.

Now, what do I do?

Every part of my life had been dedicated to protecting Emily. I made no move unless her benefit was involved. If not, I laid low and minded my business.

She's gone.

I stopped in front of the tv and stared at my hands, hoping my palms would give me an answer. I watched my chest rise and fall.

She can't be dead. My heart is still beating. My lungs are still moving. She can't be dead. How am I able to breathe without her?

My phone rang. I leaped to the coffee table and grabbed it.

Darryl's name flashed on the screen.

"Yo!" I had no patience. "What the fuck is going on?"

"Is Emily there?"

"No, and where the fuck are you at?"

His voice sounded shaky. "That's…a complicated answer."

"Have you heard about the explosion in the Financial District?"

"Yeah."

"Emily was there."

"Yeah. I figured. Rumi's lawyers are down there. The Lion would have wanted her to go there this morning—"

"Yeah, let's talk about this Lion. Why the fuck would you send him to Emily?"

"Listen, Max. You have to calm down—"

"I'm not calming down. You ended up getting me in this shit, and you know more than you're telling."

"I didn't get you into this. Emily got you into it. You're the one cleaning up her messes."

"Because her brother won't look after her."

"Oh, that's why?"

Silence hit the line.

My breathing increased. Rage blazed in my blood. I felt myself growing hot and ready to combust.

With the phone still on my ear, I turned the tv.

The distorted photo of Emily's face showed on the screen again.

Sighing, I said into the phone, "I think…I think that…she's dead."

His words were sad and low. "Me too."

I closed my eyes and tried to shut the agony away. "Where are you?"

"It doesn't matter. We have some shit to take care of first, and then we'll meet up."

"What shit?"

"Where's the hooker?"

"I killed her."

An evil chuckle left him. "You didn't. You don't kill women, and you don't kill unless Emily tells you."

I opened my eyes and sat down on the couch. "I've got her somewhere."

"Why did you lie?"

"Because I don't fucking trust you right now. You sent that Russian to Emily and now she's dead right along with him. Too convenient for you."

"What the hell would I get from doing that?"

"I don't know."

Had Emily been here I would've asked her. She'd always been good with shit like that, dissecting things before others.

"We're in this together, Max," he said it in that smooth voice he liked to use on Kennedy, when he was lying.

"Who do you think you're bullshitting?" I gripped the phone harder. "If we were in this together, then I would know what you know."

"You do."

"Fuck you, Darryl."

"Eh, whatever. Just get rid of the hooker. That's all I'm saying."

"She's long gone."

"She better be. That's the last loose end."

I stared at the phone.

The last loose end?

Darryl used to play in the chess club back, when shit had been normal. As a kid, I thought it was the most boring thing ever. I always had more fun, playing with Emily. She loved to play hide and seek, always finding the best places to disappear. The few times I found her, I would feel like the King of the World.

But now I wished I'd learned more about chess, because now I felt like I was on someone's game board, being played for a fool.

Darryl continued, "I got some money for you, Max."

"What money?"

"Chill money. Relax money. Funds to get your ass out of the city."

"I can't leave. Emily might not be dead. She could just be injured or—"

"She's dead, man. I don't want to believe it, but what can we do?"

"Be hopeful."

"Fuck hopeful. Get the fuck out of this city."

Why? What's going on? What aren't you telling me?

"There were Jamaicans where the bomb hit," I said.

"Yeah, I heard. I doubt it's anything."

Which means it's everything. Darryl has a connection with the Shower Posse. Now it's nothing?

"Max?"

"Yeah."

"You're going to want to get out of this city by the end of tonight. Don't be thinking about any revenge or what happened and who did this or that. Get out of here."

"That doesn't sound like a suggestion."

"I'm sorry, Max, but it's not. Get out of here. I don't want to lose someone else. Enough people have died today."

This is a check mate. I just don't know how he took my king.

"Okay, but I don't need to meet you for any money. I've got my own."

"Good. I would get out of here fast."

I clenched my jaw, not liking his insinuating threat.

"And get rid of all that Tinder Killer shit."

I glanced at my office where I'd posted on the news clippings, hoping to one day explain it all to Emily. "Yeah. I guess. . .I don't need it anymore."

"Exactly. It's time to move on."

Your sister just died. You don't care? You don't want revenge like me?

He continued, "In a way, Emily's death worked everything out."

I drowned in anger. "How so?"

"Now, we don't have to clean up her shit."

The phone hung up. No goodbye or wishes for a safe trip. Just a subtle threat to leave Emily's murder alone and get the fuck out of New York.

He played me. He fucking played us all.

Chains clinked in my bedroom. I'd put the hooker in there. The Russians and Emily had been keeping me busy. I still wasn't sure what I would do with her.

Darryl was right about one thing. No one else needs to die today.

There was a duffle bag on the coffee table full of money. I'd taken it out to give some of the money to the hooker. I grabbed two huge stacks. Several thousand in each hand.

I must get her out of here, before Darryl gets someone to kill her. He's behind this. I know it.

I headed to the door and opened it.

Her eyes widened. She tried to scream under the duct tape.

"Hey, don't." I kept my hands in the air, showed her the thick stacks of cash, and slowly walked to her. "I'm not going to hurt you. In fact, I'm going to let you go."

She shook but stopped trying to scream.

"You just have to get the fuck out of here. Okay?"

She quickly nodded.

"I'm going to take the duct tape off. The shit will hurt. Then, I'm going to untie you, give you some clothes and money."

She gave me a look like she didn't believe me.

"Listen. You walked in on some shit that you weren't supposed to walk in on." I peeled the tape from her mouth.

She winced, but kept her gaze on me, remaining silent.

"I needed to make sure you wouldn't tell a certain set of guys." I threw the duct tape down and undid her rope on her hands. "Now, those set of guys are dead, and there's no reason to care about the missing hooker."

Her lip quivered. "I-I wouldn't tell anyway."

"It's nothing to tell now anyway." I guided her to set down on the bed. Her ankles were still tied. I didn't undo them yet. She probably still wasn't sure I would let her go and may escape.

She looked tired and hungry on top of being scared to death. I reached up and touched her cheek again, and she flinched. My jaw tightened.

She shook her head. I slid my fingers across her cheek, stealing another touch of her, unable to control myself.

No. Leave her alone. What are you doing? You're just sad and missing her...

"Hold on." I went to the right side of the room where I'd placed her pocket book. I set the stacks of cash inside. Still rummaging through I found her wallet and pulled out her driver's license.

"Brooklyn Thompson," I read her name. "But, you're from New Jersey."

"My mom was from Brooklyn," she whispered.

"You have to go further than New Jersey now. West Coast would be better. Jump on a plane, train, or bus." I gazed at her. "Do you have any kids?"

"No."

"Good. Then, you can disappear."

A tear left her eye. "I could."

"You will." I placed the driver's license back in her bag with the money and brought it over to her, laying it on her lap.

"I'm going to untie you, and you're going to calmly take the clothes in that chair, change, and then you can go."

She swallowed. "I can go?"

"Yes. I swear to God. I'll even leave the apartment." I pointed at her. "But I won't be far, so don't call the cops or any shit like that. Get dressed and sneak away with your head up like it's just a normal day. And then go right to a Greyhound."

"Okay."

"Get on a Greyhound to somewhere like Chicago or something. Then when you hit there, get a hotel room."

She blinked.

"Go to the store and get some dye or scissors. You either need to shave off your head or dye that shit blonde or red."

She nodded.

"Did the brothel service have your real name?"

"No."

"Then, you're good." I undid her ropes and stood. "You change your look and then go to the airport and buy a ticket. Always use cash."

She nodded again.

"Go out west. Link up with someone who can give you a new identity."

I backed away. "You got this."

She grabbed the purse and hugged it to her. "You're really letting me go?"

"Yes." I checked my watch. "I'll be back in an hour. I've got some shit I have to do."

I won't think Emily's dead, until I see her body. Whatever is left of it.

So ready to get out of there, she pulled off the big shirt I'd put on her. And she was a beautiful, curvy woman.

My cock grew painful from the sight.

I looked away, inhaling her scent one last time and walking out.

The door shut behind me. I heard a click next.

Saving and walking away from pretty women. That had been the story of my life. Not that this would've been any type of love affair. In fact, it was kidnapping, but she was still beautiful, and I was still walking away.

And it always dealt with Emily.

You can't be dead.

Darryl thought I would just rush out of New York and not look back. How could I just leave without dealing with the person who'd killed her? How could I just walk away, when she was the reason why I got up every day?

How long had I only lived for Emily?

I left my apartment and went to her door which was right across from mine. I placed my hands against the cold wood's surface as if I could feel her heartbeat come from it.

If Emily's dead, then I'll burn this place down. That's the one thing I could do for her.

Tears left my eyes as I placed both hands flat against the door. Old memories rushed back to me. Hurtful ones. Visions that kept me up at night, filled with regret.

"Come on, kids." My dad laughed as he took a swig of rum and left the bottle on the table. Other adults played cards on top of it—Emily's dad Willie, Xavier, and Kennedy's parents who were notorious for cheating at spades.

Emily's dad Willie pointed at them. "You two are signaling each other again!"

"We are not." Kennedy's mother scratched her forehead. "I just had an itch."

"Itch my ass. You're signaling your husband."

Xavier laughed. "Willie act like we're playing spades for money. Motherfucker, just tell me what you're going for. I'm tired of them beating us."

"Come on, kids." Dad stumbled around, rounding all of us up. "Yall need to get up and move around. It's been raining all day and yall been stuck in the house with all these adults."

Emily's dad Willie nodded. "Yeah. Get their butts running. Darryl and Emily will be up all night, if they don't run."

Everyone laughed, except Emily.

She'd been playing dolls with Xavier's little daughters. They'd just turned six years old. Once they heard the word "basement," they rushed down to hide.

Frowning, Emily dragged herself from the couch, kicked a doll, and fisted her hands to her sides. "I don't want to play with. . .Mr. Grady today."

Willie got so mad, spit flew from his lips. "Ain't nobody asked you, if you wanted to play with him. Get your ass over there and play, Em. Always hanging around adults and listening in on conversations. You're too damn sneaky and nosy."

"But, Kennedy is asleep." Emily pouted. "I'm tired too. Can't I just go back in her room and—"

"No, you're not. You'll just go back there and wake her up." Willie waved her away. "Go on now. Go on. All yall get out of here. Let the adults play."

Darryl and I had been playing video games. Grimacing we saved our spot and then turned it off.

Chuckling, my dad grabbed Emily's hand. "Come on, yall. It's raining outside. We'll go play hide and seek in the basement."

"No." She twisted her had away from my dad. "I don't like the way you play."

Shock covered my dad's face. "Oh, come on, Emily. Why do you say that?"

"Emily Chambers!" Willie rose from the table. "Get your ass down there. Why do you always have to make a big deal about things. You see your brother and Max do what they're told."

Darryl and I had already headed to the door leading to the basement. Our parents had known each other all their lives, growing up together and then eventually moving into the same building of brownstones as adults.

Dad tried to help Emily out. "Hey, girl, how about we grab you all some ice cream first. You and I can get it from the bodega and take it down to the basement later."

Darryl stopped in the door way. "I want chocolate."

"Vanilla!" I yelled.

Emily just glared at us and then stared at the floor. "I don't want any ice cream."

"Man, get this girl before I hurt her." Willie sat back down at the table as the other adults laughed. "I told you my wife spoiled the shit out of her."

"She'll be fine, Willie." My dad patted Emily's back and she flinched. "The poor girl is just missing her mother. That's all."

"I have to get my jacket." Emily kept her hands fisted and hurried down the hall, but I saw her stop and slip into the kitchen. Her family's kitchen had two entrances. She sneaked in and I leaned my head to the side to see what she was doing. Pulling out the silverware draw, she pulled out a steak knife.

At the time, I didn't get what she was doing. She ran out of the kitchen, hurried to her room, and came back out with her jacket folded in front of her.

She never saw me see her with that knife, and I never told anyone that she'd grabbed it.

"Be nice to Emily." My dad nodded his head at her as she got to his side.

Darryl and I walked down to waste time until Dad and Emily came back with the ice cream.

The basement door shut behind us, ending the last moments we'd had of a normal life.

Dad never brought the ice cream back. It was the last time I'd seen him alive.

Stop it.

Crying, I backed up from the door and wiped away my tears.

I hadn't thought about that day in a long time. And today wouldn't be the day where I thought about it anymore.

I had to find Emily. I couldn't live without her. And it wasn't a sex or romantic thing. And we were more than siblings could ever be. I just knew that where Emily went, I would go. And what she wanted, I would make sure she had.

She was my soul.

I must go to where the bomb happened and see what I could find out.

Chapter 13
Emily

Luka stepped inside my office, taking up most of the doorway.

"There's a dead woman in the back of the gallery," Luka said. "Still warm. We might've just missed who killed her as we were climbing up the ladder. It's a straight shot at the center of her forehead. No gun or nothing else was left behind."

"Dead woman?" I shrieked. "In my gallery?"

A surge of nausea crept up my throat. I tried to rush away to see what Luka was talking about.

Kazimir grabbed my arm. "No, you shouldn't look."

"Don't worry." I moved from his grip. "I've seen dead bodies before."

I hurried out of my office, made it to the back, and froze.

I knew who the dead woman was.

Fuck you, God.

My best friend Kennedy lay on the ground looking like a beautiful frozen doll. Blue dress and heels. Perfect makeup. Hair done up in a bun. The only indication of what had happened was the bloody hole in the center of her forehead.

All my paintings from last night lay against the wall.

"Kennedy," I whispered. My knees buckled a little. I forced myself to stand straight, but on the inside, I wanted to curl up around her and cry. I wanted to tear my hair out over and over and over again until my head ripped into silence

Kazimir walked up to her and kneeled, studying the hole. "When was the last time you seen her?"

"Last night. This morning, she was supposed to be giving the paintings to the person who commissioned the lions." My voice cracked at the end. I fisted my hands, holding the tears in, keeping the grief down in my stomach. "It was a secret buyer. She'd only talked to him on the phone."

Luka shook his head and then took his time looking at every painting. "Are all of the paintings here?"

My eyes watered.

I did a quick count. "No. They're not all here. I did twelve paintings. Kazimir took one last night. There's only ten now. Maybe the killer took the other."

Kazimir rose to his feet and walked over to me. "Which one is missing?"

I scanned each painting and then my own mind. "It was the family of lions."

"What else?" he asked.

"Why does it matter?" I hugged myself and sighed. "Sorry. It was the family of lions tearing an antelope apart. Instead of red paint, I used gems.

Luka put his gun away and rubbed his face with both hands. That didn't ease my mind. Both Kazimir and him appeared like they knew exactly what was going on. Frustration pushed away my sadness. And the reality of Kennedy being gone was a tremendous crash into my world. Part of me wanted to grab my phone and call her up, letting her know about what happened.

I'll never get to talk to her again.

I ran my fingers through my hair. This had knocked me down, and I wasn't sure when I would get back up and fight another day.

It's going to be okay. It's going to be okay.

Kazimir and Luka exchanged uncomfortable glances.

"What's going on?" I looked at Kazimir and then Luka. "What are you both thinking?"

"I need time to think about this," Kazimir said.

"My friend is dead, and the Shower Posse wouldn't have done this. Many of Kennedy's cousins are in the gang. Something else is going on, and when I find out who is behind this, I'm going to kill them."

I was going to rip their world apart like they'd done to me. Hadn't I seen enough death in my life? Hadn't I lost almost every damn person that I loved? I'd thought God and I had a deal. That since I'd suffered so much tragedy in my childhood, I would get a break as an adult.

In life, people said that everything happened for a reason. But what about death? What was the fucking reason for that? That fucked up Angel of Death enjoyed to take the young and beautiful. The innocent. The ones that people loved. Snatching souls. Breaking hearts. Upsetting the world with unexpected death.

My tortured mind drifted as my gaze fell on her dead body. Violent thoughts spun through my head.

Suddenly, I felt drunk. Intoxicated. Like I was losing my balance and close to blacking out from drinking too much liquor.

Kazimir watched me. "Luka, stay here and take care of her friend. We need some space."

Anger shadowed Kazimir's face, but I didn't care why he was getting mad. I wanted to know who'd killed my best friend—my sister—one of the few people who loved me in this city.

"Come on, Emily." Kazimir tenderly grabbed my hand and guided me away.

We left Luka in that part of the gallery and walked to the front.

Outside the sky darkened. The door had been closed and locked. The lights were off so no one walking by could see inside.

I checked the door.

The person had the key to lock up. Did they take it from Kennedy after they killed her or did the person already have it?

Kazimir squeezed my hand. "What can I do?"

"Why Kennedy?" I asked.

"I don't know yet."

I spat the words out. "Russians did this."

"Yes."

"I didn't ask. It's the same style of shot—clean and straight to the brain." I moved my hand from his. "Do all of your men shoot that way or only a few?"

"Only the ones that started off with me in the beginning."

"How many is that?"

Kazimir frowned.

My voice rose with pain. "My friend is dead. Please, answer my question."

Kazimir kept a blank expression on his face. "There are ten men that kill this way. It's called a classic shot."

"Ten?"

Kazimir lifted the side of his lip into a sneer. "Yes, ten men, but only three are here in New York right now."

"Who are they?"

"Luka, me." Kazimir clenched his teeth. "And my step brother, Sasha."

I backed up. "Your brother?"

"I thought my brother may have had a hand in this, when we were at the building today. Only Luka and he knew we were going today."

"Did Sasha know Rumi?"

"Of course. Sasha handled my business in New York from time to time. Although last night I'd realized that he'd been coming to New York more. That brothel was one of his new businesses."

"Very new. Probably two years old, but then it was so high-end it could just be out of my social circle's ears."

"No, two years sounds right."

I hugged myself, trying to warm my body from this new cold reality. "Sasha knew you would come to New York, if Rumi was dead?"

"Yes."

"And he had an easy way to kill the brothel madam because he owned the place and probably could get around without anyone noticing."

"Yes."

I sighed. "What I don't understand is why Kennedy was killed."

"The lions." He took both of my hands and pulled me into a hold. "I'm so sorry, but it was the paintings of the lions."

"The lions?" I struggled to get out of his grip. "I don't understand and let me go."

"No. You need a minute."

I looked up at him as tears brimmed on my lids.

"Take a minute to breathe, Emily. Just one. Maybe two."

Sighing, I buried myself into his chest and cried, showing my weakness, exposing it all. I had no idea it would come out like that. I'd held it in. I was doing a good job.

Kazimir wrapped his arms around me. "Sasha commissioned you to do the lions. He knows me. He knows how I am about seeing things."

My words chocked on my tears. "But, why?"

"We'll see."

I moved my head from his chest and wiped my face, refusing to break down in front of him anymore. "You can let me go now."

He did, but now concern covered his face.

I turned away from him. "I'm fine."

"No, you're not."

"I will be fine."

"I'll have my men take care of your friend and handle everything."

"You're not sure, if you have any men right now. Your brother could've gotten to them."

"Sasha always has a good start with a plan, but he never thinks of the end game." An evil smile appeared on his face. "For example, even if he did have my men here, even if he did control New York. . ." He pierced me with his gaze. "What is controlling New York to controlling the whole fucking world?"

A shiver ran through me.

"We'll go somewhere safe," he said. "I have calls to make. Reinforcements to come."

I backed away, needing to get space between him and me. I missed his arms and wanted more comfort. But there was no time for that. I had to figure out what was going on and survive.

Without saying anything, I walked away.

Kazimir must've understood my anxiousness.

Silent and patient, he followed.

"Your brother thinks you're dead," I said over my shoulder. "If I was him, I wouldn't even tell your men the plan. Perhaps, I would blame it on the Shower Posse."

"Any of my men that made it out today will point to the Shower Posse, probably not Sasha. No one would ever think he had anything to do with it."

"Yes." I walked to my office and entered. "I imagine you demand loyalty among your men."

"Yes, they've watched me kill many for lack of loyalty."

"So, it would've been difficult for Sasha to get your men to go against you?"

"More than difficult. My men know that if I find out that they've been disloyal, not only will they die, but generations of their family will too. And I never waver on that promise."

"If I was Sasha, I would've maneuvered a plan behind your back to get you killed, yet without his hands touching it." I tapped the edge of my desk. "And I would stay close to you the whole time. The closer I was, the less you would suspect."

Kazimir scowled. "That is what he's done. The bomb was the only time he chose to stay in his room."

"Because he knew it would go off."

"Yes."

"Family sucks."

"Yes, it does."

Minutes later, Luka came into the office. "I've put the dead woman in the refrigerator. I removed all of the shelves."

I opened my mouth in shock.

"It's to keep the smell away." Luka smiled as if he'd given me a present. That thick accent dotted each word. "This will make for a nice funeral. She has a very pretty face—"

"Luka." Kazimir placed his hands in his pockets and continued to monitor my actions, making me feel too exposed to him. Either way, just from saying Luka's name, the guard went silent.

"What's on your mind, Emily?" Kazimir asked.

"Something is off." I walked over to my desk and sat down, suddenly feeling exhausted. "If this was all planned out by your brother, then why have me involved? I don't get it."

"You were distracting me."

"But, how could he plan months ago to make sure I distracted you?"

"Your brother pointed me to you."

Darryl, you stupid fuck.

And then I sighed. "Things are starting to make more sense now."

Kazimir sat down in the chair across from my desk.

How insane that just a night ago, we'd been in my office, in the same chairs. But at that time, I'd been scared, and he was in control. Now we both sat in front of the other like equals, realizing that we'd both been played.

"The only way Sasha would've guaranteed that my brother points you to me is. . ." I didn't want to say it out loud.

Kazimir finished, "If your brother was in on this with mine from the very beginning."

"I don't want to think that way." I shook my head as anger rose inside of me. "Then it would mean my brother was trying to kill me."

"Maybe Darryl didn't know that Sasha would let you get caught in the bomb."

"Maybe." I could see that more.

Darryl was gullible and jumped the gun with half-brained ideas that always got him and I in trouble. He was always trying to get money fast, never thinking it all out for the best path to success. Always trying to show me that he could outdo me in the streets. He thought it was a competition between us whereas I was just trying to survive.

Darryl, did you have something to do with this?

"Okay." I leaned back in my chair. "If Darryl was in on this with Sasha from the beginning, then who killed Rumi?"

"Your brother?" Kazimir shrugged. "Sasha was with me, and if we're assuming that Sasha has kept this a secret from my men, then none of them would've done this."

"No, not Darryl." I shook my head. "My brother would do a lot of things, but he doesn't have the balls to kill."

"Then it wasn't him. Whoever killed Rumi was a psychotic murderer. They sliced him and then they pulled his intestines out and drew smiley faces on his—"

"What?" I sat up in my chair. "There were smiley faces on his body?"

"Yes."

Letting out an exasperated breath, I stood up.

Kazimir rose with me. "What?"

"We should go talk to Maxwell. He didn't do it, but he knows who did." I went over to my closet. Clothes packed the space. Little mannequin heads were on the top shelf covered in various wigs. I pulled out a hanger with jeans and a shirt. "I need a minute to change. Could you leave the room?"

"I trust you, Emily, but I'm not leaving you alone." Kazimir gestured for Luka to go.

Luka left and shut the door.

Kazimir turned back to me. "You can change in front of me."

I frowned. "I won't slip away."

Kazimir studied all the other clothes in the closet and then stared at the mannequins' heads covered in wigs. "But you could slip away, if I left the office."

"I could, but—"

"Change."

I frowned, placed my back to him, and tried to unzip the back of my dress.

"I must be careful." His hands appeared on my back, moving mine out of the way and held the zipper. "You've become very special to me. You've saved my life and helped me figure out what's going on."

It was hard to think with him so close to me. "I like my privacy."

Slowly, he slipped the zipper down. With each inch, the dress opened. He let the zipper go and the material flapped to the sides, ready to fall off my arms. "You'll get your privacy back, when our brothers stop killing people."

"Good point."

He brushed his fingers along the length of my spine. "I'm sorry about your friend."

For some reason, I closed my eyes, not even wanting to change my clothes or go pursue these questions that had filled my minds.

Kazimir walked around me. "I'll keep you safe and help her family. My men will take care of everything—her body, the funeral—everything."

I opened my eyes. "Thank you."

And then my damn eyes watered again. I'd thought I had the whole thing under control. At least, if Kazimir had left the office, I would've had enough time to cry.

"You two were very close?" he asked.

"I considered her my sister." A tear fell. I hurried and wiped it away. I was shattered and feeling helpless. It wasn't a sensation I enjoyed at all, especially in front of him.

"Come here," Kazimir said.

Shocked, I looked up and wiped my eyes. "What? I'm fine. I just needed a minute."

"Perhaps, you need more than a few minutes." He wrapped his arms around me. Hard muscle caged me in, and instead of feeling trapped, I felt protected and no longer alone in this shitty world.

For seconds, maybe more, I buried my face into his chest and breathed him in. When the time hit close to a minute, I backed away. "I'm good."

Concern decorated his face, but he said nothing.

I had to get Kennedy's death off my mind, if only for a few minutes. "So, you're going to watch me change?"

The question caught him off guard as he blinked and then shifted his expression back to neutral.

"I can turn around," he said.

But then where would the fun be in that?

I swallowed down my sadness and let the drug of sex lure me in. That was what I needed. I'd been full of anxiety since Kazimir walked this problem into my life. I'd had no one to relieve me, no one to help me forget about the pain.

And now with everything going on, I tip toed on the edge.

I won't fuck him. I'll just. . .

Done with thinking it through, I pulled the dress off my shoulders.

Shock and exhaustion mingled inside of my chest. I'd just escaped out of danger earlier, traveled Russians through one of my tunnels, just to find my best friend dead in my own gallery. All I wanted to do now was lay in bed.

And with how I tended to mourn, I wouldn't have minded lying in bed with Kazimir, fucking the pain away, getting Kennedy's memories out of my head so I wouldn't hurt no more.

The dress slipped down my body and dropped to the floor.

Kazimir grunted and kept his eyes on my face. He didn't even sneak a look at my body as he handed me the jeans off the hanger. "Why are you changing?"

"Because we should go back through the tunnels." I stepped into my jeans one leg at a time. "I like that everyone thinks that we're dead. Now, they'll chill out and stop trying to kill us."

"I agree." He stepped closer to me.

I grabbed the jean's zipper to finish putting on my jeans.

Blocking my actions, Kazimir placed his hands on the top of mine and zipped my pants up, buttoning them at the top. "Do you always have a change of clothes in your office?"

"Tons of them." I grabbed my shirt.

His fingers still lingered at the top of my jeans. They never moved. Hot sex radiated off him. So close, I found it difficult to put on my shirt.

"Are you okay?" he whispered.

"I will be." I pulled the shirt over my head and put it on.

Still, his hands remained on the top of my jeans, even as the bottom of the shirt touched his palms. "Whatever you need, I will give you. Did Kennedy have—"

"I don't want to talk about Kennedy anymore." I sighed.

"Okay."

"And. . .I will need. . .something."

"Tell me and I will give it to you, Emily."

Should I? Do I even have the time? Is this crazy?

Studying his handsome face, I placed my hands on his as he still touched my jean's button. My world was spinning and somehow, I hoped his hands could anchor me.

"Once we get answers," I said. "I want you to take care of me. . ."

Kazimir's thick accent lowered to a soft groan. "Take care of you?"

It was hard to ask. Especially since I was feeling crazy and sad at the same time. "Sex is like a drug for me. It makes me high. It helps me forget things that I don't want to remember."

Gripping the top of my jeans harder, he slowly pulled me to him. "I'll do that and more, Emily. Whatever you need. Let's get your answers and then I'll *take care of you*. Later, we'll get my answers, and pray that Harlem survives."

He licked his lips. "And whether Harlem makes it or not, I'll take care of you again."

And I realized that for these few moments—I didn't have to change into new clothes. I didn't have to outthink or outsmart anyone. I could simply shed my clothes and leave this reality. Run away from these problems and sad thoughts.

For these few moments, I could just get lost in him.

Chapter 14
Kazimir

Standing just inches from her, I touched her bottom lip with my thumb, thinking about how sweet her kisses were and what they did to me.

Her office's soft, muted light graced the contours of her cheekbones and full lips.

"That sounds good." Emily didn't move my hands from her jeans, and her face didn't show relief after what I'd said. She was in pain, suffering from the mourning of her friend and the possible deceit of her brother.

And how am I, knowing that my step brother tried to kill me? I'm not happy at all. I need to fuck my anger away.

Tears collected along the rims of her eyes. She turned away as if hiding her pain.

Don't hide it from me, mysh.

I stroked her cheek, forcing her to look at me. "It will be okay, Emily."

"Is it ever okay?"

"Yes."

"Then, you've been luckier than me."

"Good. Then, I can show you the way." Something hot and heavy collected in my gut. I got this urge to protect her from anything and everything. Due to today's events, I was too edgy, too anxious, and too ready to fuck all the craziness away.

And I had to fuck Emily.

It was the only way to clear my head and get me back to where I needed to be.

And she craved it just as much as me. I could see it in her eyes and the way she arched her back, pushing those full breasts in the air. Then, she changed in front of me. I hadn't looked, but it was enough to drive me off the ledge. My balls were heavy and hungry for release. And my cock wanted to be deep inside of her.

She inched closer to me. "Thank you."

I hated how sad and weak she sounded. Her friend had been killed. Her brother possibly deceived her. Death and betrayal. Those were things I understood.

Oh, mysh. Don't worry. I'll show you how to navigate through pain.

Not thinking, I kissed her, trying to suck all her hurt away. I moved my hands from the front of her jeans and slipped along her hips, cupping her fat ass in my hands.

"I could take care of you now, if you need it." I squeezed the softness of her ass. "*I* damn sure need it."

A moan was her only response.

I was sure Luka heard it outside of the office door. How he must've thought I was a mad man.

After everything that occurred the last thing I needed to be doing was fucking. But sex would happen, because my body ached just like hers, and my heart ached too. And the only thing that could stop the pain in my chest was filling Emily with my cock, going deep inside of her and getting lost.

I glared at the door, wishing I could lock it with my mind. I didn't want to let go of her to shut it. But I didn't want Luka to walk in on me fucking Emily. Because she would be spread out on that desk, naked and taking all of me. And no one should see that beautiful vision but me.

"Please, help me forget everything for a few moments." She kissed me back.

"Oh, Emily, it may be more than a few moments." My cock hardened in my pants. I'd been ready for her hours ago, when she first walked to my limo.

I guided her back to her desk and she undressed, truly exposing herself. At first, her jeans and shirt dropped to the floor.

A beautiful gold heart locket sat on her lovely cleavage.

She'd worn a violet bra and matching panties. French lace trimmed silk. And she knew what she did to me. She had to. In those panties I could see the outline of her pussy. Plump and sweet. The softest place on earth. I yearned to be buried inside her soon. My mouth watered at the thought.

I raised my hands to her bra, touched the front clasp, and then raked my fingers over the delicate fabric, toying with her, making her ache for what could come next. My fingers caressed the bare skin at the hollow of her throat before sliding down to the tops of her breasts.

I yearned to touch her so badly. She sucked in a breath, causing her chest to rise, and I swore she extended her breasts to me, craving more of my touch.

Shivering under my fingers, she watched my reaction probably getting off on the power. How many other women could have me this out of control?

No one else. Let's hope she doesn't know.

"I need this." She moved my hands, undid the bra's clasp, and let it slip down her body and onto the desk. Chocolate nipples floated on brown pillowy breasts. Studying me, she touched her nipples with both hands, just for several sweet seconds and it caused a hitch in my throat.

I wanted her to hurry up with undressing. I needed to rip those panties away, but I'd already lost control. She didn't need to see the evidence of my impatience.

She slid her panties off next and tossed them at me. They flew over my shoulder. I couldn't keep my smirk away.

Dangerous. So dangerous.

And once again, I saw her for the first time—young, soft, and delicate. All those wigs and outfits were just distractions—ways she'd tried to protect herself. Underneath she was fragile. Stripped bare, she could be bruised and hurt.

This one has so many layers, and I just want to take my time lifting every one of them.

"I'll take care of you, Emily." I captured her soft body into my hands and placed her further on top of the desk. "Anything you need, I'll be there."

Underneath hooded eyes, she gazed at me. "I just want you to fuck me."

That triggered a grunt.

"I'll fuck you too. I'm going to bury my cock deep inside you."

"Please."

I caressed her soft skin, relishing my first touch of her. She was even softer than I thought. Even more delicate. Unable to stop myself, I spread her legs apart. A beautiful view greeted my eyes. She had no hair between her thighs, just a lush opening.

Hunger lathered her words. "Take your cock out."

"I don't usually take orders, but for you, I will." The tip of my cock throbbed in anticipation. I opened my pants and let them drop to my ankles.

As if impatient, she raised her hands to my shirt and yanked it open. My buttons sprayed the desk. Then she's touching my waist and raking her nails over the hard-tattooed ridges of my abs, taking the time to feel each and every mound of muscle.

Grunting, I dove my hands into my boxer briefs and pulled my cock out.

She'd been focused on my chest and yanking the shirt down my biceps, but my cock had caught her attention. Her hands left my shirt, as she caressed the jutting thickness of my cock, lingering her fingertips at the mushroomed tip.

"This is what I need." She traced my shaft and then slipped her fingers to my balls, cupping them both in her palms.

I groaned in pleasure, not giving a fuck if the whole world crumbled around me. Sasha and whoever could do whatever. All that mattered in this moment was her pussy and the fastest way that I could slip inside of her sweet flesh.

I yank off my shit and threw it on the floor.

Her gaze went to the lion tattooed on my arm. "Beautiful."

And then she shocked me and spat on my cock.

Stunned, I gazed down at the saliva, dripping along the hard length.

She spat on it some more, fisted both hands around my cock, and stroked the wet length in a punishing rhythm, driving me fucking crazy.

Dangerous.

The whole time she stared at me, looking me right in my eyes, completely in control. My cock in those slick, wet hands, tugging and squeezing, slipping and sliding.

She squeezed the thickness, prolonging the needy ache.

A low groan left me. "Emily."

She stroked her wet hands down the length again and then trailed one of her fingers along the thick pulsing vein underneath the taut skin. And I was throbbing in her palms, close to begging her to put me out of my misery.

Grunting out a curse, I cupped her breasts, toying with her nipples, loving how they pebbled under my fingertips. Both of our breathing increased, inhaling and exhaling together and with the beat of her strokes. Almost as if the sex gave us the air to breathe.

It was so good, her touching me, exploring the most intimate part of me. Continuing to fist fuck my cock, she cupped my balls with the other hand, driving me further over the edge.

"Yes." She twisted her hand around my cock with each stroke, and then gently pulled, milking it, triggering intense pleasure.

And still she watched me under hooded eyes. I could feel her seeping into my soul, getting inside of me and soaking up my warmth as if she was cold and starving.

Dangerous.

"No." I stopped her hand, right as pre-cum beaded at the top. "Lay down."

Emily's eyes went wild. Her pouty lips parted a fraction, as if she wanted to say something to me, but couldn't. I swore she gasped or maybe she moaned. I was so lost in her I couldn't compute what was going on.

She panted as if jacking me off had been getting her hot. Her pussy surely said so. As she lay down and spread her legs even wider, wetness saturated her clit and drenched her folds. Those puffy lips were smeared with cream and I wanted to lick it off, suck on that pussy, making her cum from my mouth.

I rubbed more of her arousal all over her puckered clit, making slow circles around the bud.

As badly as I yearned to be balls deep inside her, I needed to make this last. We deserved this moment. We'd averted a bomb and won over those that tried to hurt us. We'd survived. And she'd helped. And damn if she didn't deserve to be fucked. She needed to remember this moment, and that it was I who dominated her.

Letting her head fall back, she gripped the edge of the desk. "Kaz."

"Kaz? I like that. You can call me that more as you moan." I dipped my finger inside of her.

Moaning, she clenched her sex on my fingers.

"Oh, Emily." I moved my hand and licked my fingers, loving the taste of her. "Your pussy's going to feel so good."

My mouth ached to suck on her clit, but my cock was impatient. He would not wait anymore.

Panting, she said, "I have condoms in here."

She tapped the drawer next to my leg with her foot.

I opened the drawer and raised my eyebrows. "There's at least six boxes of condoms in here."

"I like to be safe."

But how safe do you need to be? How many men?

The thought of another man pushing his dick inside of her made me ready to kill someone. I grabbed a box out and glared at her.

She slipped her hands up to her breasts and pinched her own nipples. "Why are you frowning at me?"

"I should warn you." I tore open a condom and pulled it out the wrapper. "I can be possessive."

She widened her eyes. "Are you always possessive with the woman you fuck?"

"No, but I will be possessive with you."

She blinked and looked like she was about to sit up and protest my statement. But her eyes went to my cock as I slid the condom on.

I gripped her thighs and guided my cock to her wet opening, not even needing my hands to hold it. "Whoever you were fucking before, you don't fuck anymore."

She opened her mouth to speak, but I fucked the answer away, thrusting hard into her.

"Kaz," she groaned.

Pumping hard and fast, I couldn't stop myself. Her pussy was heaven, lifting me out of the insanity of what this Harlem trip has become, and giving me peace for a few moments. Pleasure. Hot and doused in flames, it flowed through me, tidal waving through my body. It felt so good. Too good. Every nerve pulsed and burst.

With each deep thrust, she clenched her pussy around my length, sucking me back into her, not letting me pull away.

"Oh, little *mysh*." I leaned forward, sucking a nipple into my mouth.

She brought her hands to my head and gripped my hair, holding me tight against her.

And those beautiful brown eyes had me hypnotized. There was nothing else more important than this moment with her. Everything could crumble around us—the world itself—and I would not look away.

I captured her lips, kissing as I thrust.

Our mouths slipped smoothly against each other. Our tongues slid in perfect motion. Kissing her was easy. Touching her. Fucking her. Thrusting into her wet, warm sex. It was all easy. Tasting her tongue and hearing her moan. So easy. Like the boom of a heartbeat. Like waking up after sleep. Like I was always supposed to do it. It was so good. So fucking easy. Like breathing, and I yearned to breathe her all in—with each stroke, with each lap of my tongue. I needed to inhale her because she'd already sucked me in.

My body submerged into erotic sensation after sensation.

"Kaz, I'm coming." Her pussy squeezed my cock without mercy.

And a flame of burning desire built in me. A growing wildfire scorching everything in its path. My cock was ready to combust.

"Oh. Oh," she cried out. Her orgasm was wild and gorgeous. Savagely beautiful. So vulnerable. And I loved watching her fall apart until she was too numb to move.

Yes. Like that, Emily.

Her pussy trembled around my cock.

Fuck.

My back grew tight as my fingers gripped her hips, driving into her one last time, crawling deep inside this beautiful woman, possessing her as much as I could.

I came with her, groaning as I thrust. My vision exploded into color. My skin blazed with numb-thundering heat.

Panting, I held her in my arms. My cock still stiff and inside of her. I didn't want to let her go and face the truth—the problem I had ahead of me.

Letting out an exasperated breath, she moved out of my arms. "Thank you."

I pulled my cock out of her, slipped the filled condom off me, and threw it in the small trash can next to the desk.

Lifting her leg, she twisted around and scooted off her desk. Embarrassment flushed over her face.

"Where are you going?" I raised my eyebrows.

I want to fuck you some more.

"I'm going to clean up in the bathroom." Her ass jiggled as she hurried over to her clothes on the floor and picked them up. "We have to get back to—"

"Come back over here."

She held her clothes in front of her, shielding her nudity from me. Her gaze swept over my lips, chin, neck, and then back up to my face. "We. . .have brothers to deal with."

My chest ached. I hadn't wanted her to remind me of that. The whole point of our fucking was to forget. Now I was back to enraged and I didn't want her to see it.

"You're right." I gritted my teeth. "Go ahead and change."

What will we do with our brothers? Let's hope we've got this all wrong.

Act Three
Definition of Dirty

3: obscene and pornographic.

dirty jokes
dirty movie

Chapter 15
Maxwell

Xavier's girls raced all over the damn basement, jumping this place and that place. Still, Darryl and I got bored waiting for my dad and Emily to come down.

The little girls screamed together, "We want to play hide and seek."

"Okay." I shook my head. "You two go hide. We'll find you. Don't leave that place, when you find it. Just like Emily."

"You won't find me." One of them rushed off and the other followed on even bonier legs.

"Where is the ice cream?" Darryl slung the basketball at the wall and sighed. "I'm going up there to see what's up."

"I'm coming."

Forgetting about the girls, we raced up the stairs, knocked each other when we could, trying to see who could get to the top first.

I beat Darryl and fell into the living room as the door opened.

"Hey!" Willie yelled. "Stop all that running. Aren't yall getting enough of that down in the basement?"

"Yes, sir." I scanned the space for Dad or Emily. "We were just looking for the ice cream?"

Willie drank a beer and quirked his eyes at Xavier. "Didn't Reggie come back from the store with Emily?"

"Shit. That was a minute ago." Xavier checked his watch, set his cards down, and rose from the table. "I'll go see what's up. I'm done playing with your cheating asses anyway."

Willie pointed at Kennedy's mother. "She stays signaling."

Xavier scratched his head and headed toward the front door.

I checked outside the window. The sky had brightened where most of the day it had been dark and gloomy.

"Can we come?" I asked.

"Yeah." Xavier felt his pockets. "We need more beer anyway."

A heavy hand hit my shoulder.

I glanced behind me.

Xavier's old tired face glared as he stood behind me. "It's all over the streets. People are saying Emily is dead and those Russians too."

I turned back around and faced the building. The scent of smoke and burning hair filled the air. Even though the day was sunny, a black smog hovered over us.

News vans parked here and there.

Fire fighters hosed down burning shards of wood, trying to get control of the continuous burning that had over taken the place. Sirens blared. Crowds of others stood around, whispering and talking.

Tons of Russian men stood around too, studying all the faces in the area. Many of them looked just as confused as me as they drank the whole seen in.

"Jamaicans and Russians?" Xavier got to my side, pulled a joint out, and lit it. "This whole place is about to be a war zone in a few days."

"You can't smoke that out here, X. Don't you see all these cops around?"

"These motherfuckers too puzzled and busy to deal with me." He blew out a cloud of smoke. "Thirty people dead so far from the explosion. And with this gun fight on the outside, that totals about sixty."

There were tons of coroner vans sprawled around the area, lifting covered bodies into them. I'd got to see a few of them. They were all charred and barely in one piece.

A few people had their phones out, recording the whole thing.

"She's dead," I whispered.

Xavier laughed and smoked more of his joint. "Poor Maxwell. Sometimes you are slow as fuck."

"What are you talking about?" I grabbed the joint from him and inhaled a little. "This isn't funny."

"If anyone would know if Emily is dead, it would be me." He pulled out his phone—an old iPhone edition from years ago that he'd found and reprogrammed. He took another hit of his joint and pressed on the screen. "There she is."

Fuck. I forgot we tagged her. Shit.

The map came up on his screen. A red dot placed her at her art gallery.

Xavier winked. "Aren't you glad I put that tracker in her heart necklace?"

"Yeah. I was just scared she would find out."

"Shit. You and me both. If she ever finds out, she'd probably kill us."

"She wouldn't."

"She would and forget about it." He checked the screen, stomped the joint out, and walked off. "Go home, Maxwell. She's heading to *that building*."

Thank God. She's alive and going home.

"Eh, Xavier," I called after the old man and ran up to him.

"What?"

"Darryl was involved in this shit somehow."

Xavier grimaced. "Of course, he is."

"If you hear from him, don't tell him that Emily is alive."

"I won't." He sighed. "Although he knows about the tracker, he might come to me and check to be sure."

"He probably forgot just like me."

"I don't see how you two could forget."

"That's how busy she's kept us this year."

Xavier shook his head and walked off.

Chapter 16
Emily

I can't believe I had sex with him. Shit. I can't believe Kennedy is gone.

Once we finished with the sex, my mind was clear. Kazimir still had it fogged, but at least the pain of Kennedy's death had lessoned for a few minutes.

I'd taken Kazimir and Luka back through the tunnels, but to my route home. Luka shook his head the whole time, knowing that way was how I'd outsmarted him. Thankfully, it was dark down there and the two men couldn't see me running my fingers across my lips over and over. Each touch of my hand on my mouth reminded me of Kazimir and those heated kisses he gave me. He'd left of trace of him all over my tongue and even inside of me. The whole walk through the tunnel, I'd been trying to savor him more.

Focus. He's only going to complicate things even more.

The tunnel walk took no time.

Once we came up for air, I was disappointed to find Xavier's bus vacant. Maxwell's place showed no lights through the dark window like he'd been gone too.

Where's everyone?

We could've taken the front, but I took a different way to get into my place.

Moonlight bathed the back of my brownstone.

I stopped at the concrete steps leading to the basement door. My place was the only one that had a basement and connected to it. My parents had paid an extra three hundred for rent because of it.

I gazed down at those steps that were still stained in red—no matter how much Maxwell said I'd bleached it all away.

Kazimir got to my side. "What's wrong?"

"Nothing. I just don't like going this way." I glanced over my shoulder.

Luka hung behind us with his gun out and eyes scanning the backyard.

I turned back to the steps and gulped. "I don't want to go through the front just in case someone's watching my place."

As if sensing how uncomfortable I was, Kazimir held my hand and squeezed. "Let's go, Emily."

I took forever going down each step. Kazimir furrowed his eyebrows but said nothing right as we got to the door. My fingers shook as I put the key into the hole.

Luka grumbled. "You're not scared of dark underground tunnels, but you're scared of basements?"

Kazimir ordered, "Be quiet."

I unlocked the door and opened it.

Cold death rose from the whole place. I still hadn't renovated it. Black soot coated all the walls. It was completely empty just scattered ash and burned out things.

Luka walked in.

Still holding my hand, Kazimir guided me forward. I dragged forward.

"Where's the way upstairs?" Kazimir asked.

Trembling, I pointed to the direction of the stairs.

"Okay." He tightened his grip on me. "What happened here, Emily?"

"A. . .fire." I let out an exasperated breath and hurried to the steps, picking up my pace.

Luka ambled up the steps first.

Kazimir watched me as he led me up them. "Did someone close to you die down here?"

"You could say that." I didn't look down anymore. I kept my focus forward as Luka opened the door into my brownstone.

When we got into my apartment, I went straight to my fridge, grabbed a bottle of rum, and took two long gulps.

Both men stared at me.

I'm never doing going down there again.

I set the bottle on the counter. "You can have some, and there's beer in the fridge too."

Luka leaned his head to the side. "Vodka?"

Kazimir frowned. "Go check the place, Luka. You don't need anything to drink."

I shrugged and took another gulp.

Kazimir grabbed the bottle from my hands and took his own swallow. "Who died down there?"

I reached for the bottle.

He moved it from me. "You were scared. I didn't like it."

"I'm fine now." I stared at the bottle.

"I don't like secrets."

"Cool." I grabbed the bottle from him and backed up, before he could get it again. "And since we're sharing secrets, then you can tell me why your step brother wants to kill you."

He leaned on the counter and smiled at me. "You're bolder now. Less scared of me."

"Should I fear you?"

"Why were you scared in the basement?" Kazimir walked over to me and took the bottle back. "We're partners now."

"You don't need me as a partner. You have countries that would back you." I took a gulp and let the liquid burn my throat. I coughed. "Why haven't you called anyone yet to. . .I don't know. . .do Bratva things."

His lips curved. "Bratva things? I like that."

He took a swig of the rum and handed it back to me. "When you're in power, there's no need to rush to move. It's always smart to sit back and observe. I'm dead now."

"True."

He winked at me. "Let's see what happens, while I'm dead."

I took my last sip, already feeling a little tipsy. "I haven't eaten. I'm hungry."

I set the bottle on the counter. "Are you hungry?"

"Yes."

"Luka too?" I asked.

"He's always excited to eat." Kazimir dove into his jacket and pulled out his wallet. "We can order—"

"No. I'm dead too." I winked back at him. "Let's see what happens. That means no deliver, and no major lights on in the house."

The curtains were already drawn and covering the windows. I grabbed tons of candles from my pantry and lit them. Luka helped me place them throughout the place.

A dim lighting bathed the space.

I gave Luka the tv. He'd been stuck to it all last night as he watched me, and I'd researched what buildings to wash Kazimir's money with. Now it all seemed like weeks ago, when that happened. For some reason spending hours in the tunnel with people made us close.

"Thanks." Luka crashed onto the couch. "You're a good person, Emily."

"Does that mean you'll never kill me?"

"As long as Kazimir doesn't ask, I can guarantee it."

I laughed. "I'll take that."

He turned the tv on. The news played on most channels. We all gathered in the living room and watched the craziness on the screen.

"The death toll for the Financial District Bombing has reached seventy-five people." The woman's hair whipped around her in the wind. Police lights flashed behind her. A large crowd stood behind yellow tape, waving at the cameras.

She gestured back to the clouds of smoke coming out of the crumbled building. *"The mayor had announced that the New York Exchange will be closed as well as other surrounding businesses and schools within a five-mile radius. A list is provided on News 9's website."*

A photo image of Luka, Kazimir, and I walking into the building appeared on the screen.

"Holy shit," I muttered under my breath.

"Authorities ask that you contact the number below, if you recognize the woman in this photo and/or know any information pertaining to these people." The image changed to black and then she returned to the screen explaining Kazimir and Luka's impressive criminal backgrounds.

But most importantly we learned that everyone assumed we'd died in the fire. Footage showed from a street light of us going inside and then five minutes later, it all exploded.

A sketch of a white man showed on the screen.

"A recent witness has come forward on the Tinder Killer, offering a description of the man's face. The witness described the man as Caucasian, around six feet, and possibly having a bear. If you see this man, please contact—"

Luka switched to another channel showing the bombing. It hadn't been hard. Tons of channels covered the tragedy. I imagined the whole world was watching this, posting hashtags on social media for all the people that had innocently died.

Kazimir shook my head. "If you didn't take us into the tunnels, then we would've died. No one would've survived that."

"That's what your step brother was hoping for." I shook my head and went to the kitchen. "If I was going to try and kill you, a bomb would be a good solution. Who would be bold enough to try and get close to you with a gun or knife."

"A sniper would be better," Luka added. "A bomb is too messy, and it kills more people than intended."

"Food poisoning is the way." Kazimir walked over to the kitchen and sat on a stool next to the breakfast bar. "I like your place."

I took out bowls and things to cook. "Thank you."

Bored with the bombing news, Luka changed the channel to a football game and placed his feet on my coffee table. I almost told him to take them down and remembered the big guns on him, and our new little friendship.

"Any food allergies?" I asked.

Kazimir chuckled. "No."

"Any type of food that you hate?"

"No, which is why food poisoning would be a good way to kill me."

"Well, I would rather not talk about that." I went to the small radio on my kitchen counter and switched it on. Slow jazz played through the speakers.

"Who died in the basement?"

I dropped a plate. It crashed to the floor.

Luka was already at the edge of my kitchen with his gun pointed at me.

I froze.

"Sorry. I thought someone was coming through the window." Luka put the gun down and went back to the couch.

"Jesus," I murmured and grabbed the broom from the pantry.

Kazimir rose and took the broom away. "Tell me."

"Why?"

"Because we don't have secrets anymore."

"Secrets are okay."

"Not between us." Kazimir swept up the plates. "And for your question earlier, Sasha—my step brother—wants to kill me because he believes that I took his position—*his father's empire*."

Kazimir walked over to the trash can and dumped the pieces.

I can now cross out "Russian mafia boss cleaning my kitchen" on my bucket list.

Kazimir set the broom on the side. "The Bratva pick you. These are killers. People I would never want you alone with. These men follow who scares them, and Sasha doesn't scare them."

"Why not?"

"Because he's gay. Some men see that as a weakness."

"Do you?"

"No. Sasha was more than capable of running the Bratva. The only problem is that he wouldn't be able to keep his reign. He's good with schemes, but never with the long run. He doesn't think big enough."

I pulled out some pots. "He's a sprinter like my brother. He comes up with a good con, but never thinks about what he'll do with the reward."

"Yes." Kazimir sat down on the stool. "My men won't be ruled by Sasha. They would've thought foul play, if I died."

"So, it's just a matter of time, when chaos begins for Sasha?"

"Yes. For now, I'll decide what I will do." He rested his elbows on my counter and knitted his fingers. "Who died in your basement?"

I put the pot down and crossed my arms over my chest. I felt like I needed to protect myself as I answered. I had to guard my body. "Two little girls died in the basement."

"And who died on the outside? You looked like there were ghosts everywhere."

"Why do you care?" I asked.

"You weren't scared in the tunnels."

I turned around and started cutting vegetables. "Maxwell's dad died by the steps of the basement."

"How?"

I banged the pot against the counter, exhaled, set it down, and turned to him. "This is not what I want to talk about."

Of course, Luka stood in the doorway with his gun pointed my way.

I glared at the big guy. "And would you please calm down?"

Kazimir nodded at him.

Luka returned to the couch.

"He's fucking fast." I gritted my teeth. "I can never hear when he comes up."

"That's the point." Kazimir kept a calm expression on his face. "Why does this make you so mad? What happened to you?"

"You should've been a therapist, instead."

"You're snappy, when you're uncomfortable."

"I don't like telling my secrets."

"You shouldn't. People can use them against you, but I won't."

"How can I tell?"

"You saved my life. Now, I want to wipe out everything that scares you, starting with this basement. Who do I have to kill? Why did you get so scared?"

I opened my mouth in shock and then shook my head. "Don't worry. I already killed him."

His eyebrows furrowed. "Maxwell's father?"

"Yes."

"The guy that you said would kill for you?"

"Yes."

"I don't understand why he's so loyal."

Fine. Just tell him everything. It doesn't matter.

I turned away from Kazimir and went back to cooking. "Maxwell's father was a good-looking guy. People called him a playboy. My father and him were best friends since they wore diapers. They all lived in this building. We all lived here, in fact."

"So, you grew up here?"

"Yes."

He rose and began to walk around as if trying to learn more about me.

"They were all friends. My parents. Kennedy's parents, Max's dad. Max's mother left them before I could walk so I don't remember her. Either way, they used to come to our place and play cards every Saturday night." I filled the pot with water. "I hated Saturdays. Still hate them."

"Why?"

"Because, after a while Maxwell's dad Reggie would wander off from the adults and always come play with the kids." I stirred the pot. "And. . .he always touched me. . ."

Hot steam rose and burned my hand. I kept my fingers there to feel the pain of the burn, wishing that the sting would be enough to erase the past.

I didn't know how long I stayed there, hurting myself.

Out of nowhere, Kazimir appeared behind me and moved my hand away.

"I can't hear, when you move either," I whispered as he pressed his body against me, pulling me away from the stove completely.

"That's the point, little *mysh*." He turned me around. "I'll send Luka for food."

Kazimir shut the stove off and placed the pot in the sink.

And even crazier, Luka had already been standing there, holding his gun to his side. "Is she okay?"

Am I okay?

"She's fine." Kazimir guided me around the bar. "She just zoned out."

I quirked my eyebrows. "What do you mean I zoned out?"

"For close to three minutes, I called your name."

That didn't make any sense. It only seemed like a minute had gone by.

Kazimir handed Luka several bills. "Get us something to eat that's close by. Go out through the basement and come back the same way."

Luka grimaced. "Kazimir, I don't like leaving you here—"

Kazimir frowned. "Get some tampons for yourself too, while you're out."

Grumbling, Luka rolled his eyes, took the money, and left.

Kazimir turned my way.

"Women are strong too," I said.

"What made you think I didn't know that?"

"The tampon comment."

"Good point." He pulled his arm in front of me and studied it. "You burned yourself."

I tried to move it away. "I'll be fine. What was I doing?"

"Just holding your arm over the steam."

I ran my fingers through my hair. "I'm fucking losing it."

"Maybe, you need to lay down."

"No." I grabbed his hand. "Maybe, I just need to fuck."

He didn't move as I tried to pull him to my room.

I blew out a long breath. "What?"

"This is all connected."

"What is all connected?"

"You. It all comes back to you for some reason. Too many meaningful coincidences. Everything keeps going back to you."

"It really doesn't." I stomped off to the bedroom, completely not feeling like myself. I needed a shower and more rum. This wasn't me. I stayed in control. I unraveled in darkness and silence.

Kazimir followed me into my bedroom and closed the door. "You killed Maxwell's father because he touched you?"

Jesus. He's not going to let this go.

"Yes, even though that day hadn't been the first time." I turned his way and hugged myself. "But my father never believed me. He beat me, when I told him, said that lying like that could get his best friend in jail. Reggie was a playboy. He couldn't believe that this guy surrounded by all these women would inappropriately touch a ten-year-old girl."

"And what did your mother say?"

"She passed from diabetes, before all of this happened."

"So, it was just you and your brother Darryl?"

"Yes, and my brother didn't believe me either. He made me swear not to tell Maxwell." I began to pace in front of my bed.

I'd never said any of this out loud before. Those that were close to me already knew the story and were trying to forget.

"That day, Reggie made me go get ice cream with him. My dad wouldn't let me stay. Everyone thought I was being a brat." I stood in the center of the room. "Instead of going to the bodega, he took me around the building to the back of the house."

"Where the steps led?"

"Yes. He kept saying that he really loved me and that him loving me would be a good thing to help me get over my mother. That it would heal me."

Rage covered Kazimir's face. If Reggie had been alive, I was sure Kazimir would've killed him.

"Reggie dragged me down the steps, pushed me against the door. . . and I don't remember much else."

Kazimir widened his eyes.

"My Uncle Xavier found me by that door sitting next to Reggie. His penis was out. Reggie was laying on the ground and there was a broken bottle sticking out of his stomach. And blood was all over me. On my face, shirt, feet, hands. . ." I gulped and closed my eyes.

Kazimir wrapped his arms around me.

"Xavier put two and two together. And what I didn't say was that our families didn't have regular jobs. They all did illegal things. Calling the cops to handle something like that wasn't even an option. Xavier was drunk, but he acted fast, he opened the basement door. We all dragged Reggie inside."

"Who is we?" Kazimir asked.

"Oh. . .my brother. . .and Maxwell had been with Xavier. Maxwell didn't even look at me as they carried Reggie inside." I buried myself into Kazimir's arms, trying to hide myself. "There used to be an incinerator in the center of the entire building where everyone lived. The basement had one opening for it. Xavier shoved Reggie's dead body in that incinerator. It blocked something—gas I don't know, but a fire exploded from there. We all raced out of there."

I climbed out of Kazimir's arms, not wanting to be comforted. "Xavier's little girls were hiding in the basement. Xavier and I didn't know. They died immediately."

Kazimir's expression looked so sad and I didn't want him to pity me.

"The fire rose to my parents' level and ate my father up. Thank God Kennedy's parents had already ended the card game and grabbed Kennedy. They'd gone off to their own place upstairs and were safe from the fire."

Kazimir stepped to me.

"No. I don't want to be hugged." I waved him away. "Xavier's wife came home an hour later. She never forgave him for dumping the body in the incinerator and starting the fire."

Sighing, I gestured outside to the alley across from us. "A month later, Xavier moved into an abandoned school bus and put a sign outside the door."

"What did it say?" Kazimir asked.

"The sign said, 'I give up.'" My eyes burned, but I wouldn't cry. "Now, will you stop asking questions and just fuck me?"

"Is that how you deal with pain?"

"Yes."

"I don't like to see you in pain." He closed the distance between us. "I'm sorry about what happened to you."

"I'm sure things have happened to you too."

"You're right, but I'll show you my wounds another day." He kissed me.

And then a boom came from the living room.

Chapter 17
Kazimir

I put Emily behind me. "That's not Luka. We would've never heard him come in. Do you have a gun?"

"Yes, but I don't use it." Emily pointed to her night stand, rushed over, pulled it out, and gave it to me.

She handed me a .38 special. The revolver caliber was a *great middle of the road* round. Good for self-defense, but packed less punch than its larger cousin, the .357 Magnum.

I checked for bullets and was satisfied. "Stay here."

She didn't argue.

More booms sounded from the living room. Whoever had come into her place didn't think anyone else was inside. They sounded like they were ransacking the house.

I slowly turned the knob and creaked the door open.

Two men rummaged through Emily's living room. Dreadlocks topped their heads. Another man was in the kitchen yanking out drawers.

Emily peeked with me and then hissed as she whispered, "They're looking for my money. My brother must've told them about it."

"Well. . .they'll wish he hadn't." I opened the door, before she could say anything else.

None of the three looked up. Escaping from jail as many times as I had, gave me the skill of moving without notice.

I went for the easiest guy first. The one in the kitchen. With one bullet, I shot him right in the forehead, no need to show off or waste more bullets than necessary.

I ducked behind the breakfast bar, knowing at least one of them would shoot at me.

The motherfucker must've had an AK-47. Bullets sprayed my way. It was a weapon for an unskilled person who couldn't get their target. Something to kill fast without any real ability. When he rested, probably thinking I was done, I shot him in his forehead. Simple and easy. No need for all the noise.

He dropped to the floor.

His friend screamed, "You blood clot motherfuck—"

A boom came his side, and then a slam as if his body crashed to the floor. I waited. Everything had gone silent.

I jumped out, aiming my gun at a new man who held a shotgun in the center of the living room.

Who's he?

This man was brown skinned but didn't have dreadlocks and it looked like he'd just killed the guy.

My finger touched the trigger but didn't pull back. "Who are you?"

"Maxwell. You're the Russian that was with Em earlier." His hand shook a little as he pointed the gun my way. "Where is she?"

"In the bedroom."

He sneered. "Alive?"

"Yes."

We kept our guns pointed at each other.

"Those were Shower Posses guys," Maxwell said.

"Yes."

"I don't know why they were here."

I nodded. "Emily had some theories."

Frowning, Maxwell tapped his finger on the gun's trigger. His hand no longer shook. "Are we supposed to kill each other or something?"

"From what Emily says, you're her friend. Extremely loyal."

"I am." He kept his gun steady. "I'm even more loyal, when a gun isn't pointed at me."

"Then, put your gun down."

He did, and I followed.

Emily rushed out of the room. "Max, are you okay?"

"Why the fuck didn't you answer your phone?" he asked.

She went up to him and just as I thought she would hug him, she kept a foot between them and hugged herself. Concern covered her face. "My phone went out in the tunnels and then I was going to charge it at the gallery, but...Kennedy..."

"What about Kennedy?" He squinted his eyes and set the gun down.

"She's dead, Maxwell."

He hit the wall behind him. "Who did it?"

"I don't know. I think it was Kaz's step brother."

Maxwell turned my way. "Kaz?"

She cleared her throat. "Kazimir."

"You two are best buddies now?" Maxwell gestured to me. "What's going on, Em?"

"You should tell me." She crossed her arms over her chest. "Why did you put smiley faces on Rumi's dead body?"

All anger fell from his face. "I-I..."

"You're about to stutter yourself into a lie." She stepped closer to him. "Don't. Just tell me what you know. Everything is going to be fine."

"Now's not the time for that conversation, but I'll tell you later."

"Now's definitely the time," she insisted.

"Yo." He covered his face with his hand and then moved them away. "There's a lot we need to talk about. We just need to do so...privately. Not here."

I stalked forward. "No. We don't keep secrets among friends."

"You're not my friend." Maxwell got between him and Emily like that would be enough to stop me. "Emily and I need to talk at my place."

I shook my head. "No."

Emily walked around Maxwell. "I'm sorry, Max, but Kazimir is right."

"He's right?" Maxwell frowned. "What the fuck happened to you in the tunnels?"

Not letting her answer, I smiled. "We bonded. Now, tell me who killed Rumi?"

"That's not an answer we need to get into right now," Max countered.

"This is bullshit." Emily pointed at him. "If we all put together what we know, then this will be over. Just fucking say it. Who. Killed. Rumi?!"

Maxwell leaned against the wall and glared at her. "You did, Em. You killed him."

"What?" She swayed to the side.

"You did." Max stepped closer to her. "I swear to God you did. You just don't remember."

"No. No." She kept blinking her eyes. "That's. . .no."

"I swear it." Maxwell raised his hands in defeat. "You killed him."

"I didn't." Her hands shook at her sides.

"You don't remember." Maxwell stalked after her. "You did it."

And then Emily passed out.

I reached for her, but Maxwell grabbed her first, right before she could hit the floor.

"She'll be okay." He studied her. "She does this all the time."

"Why did she pass out?" I asked.

Maxwell lifted Emily in his arms and carried her past me. "That's how she copes. Her brain just shuts off and reboots, when things get too hard."

That didn't make sense to me. "She didn't pass out in the tunnels or when she saw her friend's dead body."

"She's not scared in the tunnels and she's not afraid of dead bodies either." Maxwell carried her toward her bedroom like he'd done this, many times before. "She was probably anxious and freaked out, but that's not what this is."

"And this is?" I followed him into her bedroom.

"Her not being able to deal with a part of who she is. When the truth is in her face, she passes out."

"And the truth is?" I asked.

"She's a killer."

"And she doesn't know?" I asked.

Maxwell glanced over his shoulder at me. "Not as much as she should."

I remembered in the story that she said she'd passed out when she'd killed Maxwell's father. "How many times does this happen?"

"Too many fucking times." Maxwell gently placed her on the bed and sat on the edge, staring at her.

I watched him, not enjoying how he studied her, almost drinking in every feature. His fingers twitched at his sides like he yearned to touch her.

He could be a problem.

"Do you love Emily?" I asked.

"It doesn't matter." Maxwell rose from the bed. "She would never love me."

"Because of your father?"

Annoyance flickered across his face. "She told you about that?"

"Yes."

"All of it?"

"I know about her first kill and the fire in the basement."

"Her first kill." He snorted without any humor. "I guess you were right."

"About what?"

"You two did bond." Maxwell glared at me. "And have you had sex with her?"

I didn't usually answer a question like that, but I felt bad for this guy. He'd grown out of tragedy and it didn't seem like things would be getting better for him. If he got in my way, when it came to Emily, I would kill him.

And what do I want to do with Emily?

I hadn't decided, but I knew the time was coming up for me to leave New York. I'd learned enough and was close to why I'd come—finding out who killed Rumi. I'd just learned that Emily might've done it. I didn't know Maxwell. It could all be a lie, but still I had to hear him out.

But what will I do with her?

When I connected the dots to why Sasha chose Emily to be my washer, then I would leave New York. There was no need to fight him in this city. He figured I was dead, and if I survived he'd have the little Jamaican gang to come after me.

Sasha was such a small thinker, not understanding that I had more resources than him—Presidents on speed dial. Had I not cared about America, I could've sent a fucking nuke to that brothel in the sky and leveled the Manhattan island and much more.

New York can thank Emily for saving it.

Maxwell waited for the answer and so I nodded.

"Yes, we've had sex," I admitted.

Maxwell moved his finger on his side as if he wished he had a gun. "Are you going to kill her?"

I raised my eyebrows. "Why would I?"

"She killed Rumi?"

That wouldn't be enough for me to hurt her, not with all that we've gone through.

"According to you, she did it." I shrugged. "But why did Emily kill Rumi?"

"It's hard to explain." Maxwell walked out of the bedroom. "If you see the footage, you'll understand."

"You're the one that took the security cam footage?"

"Yes."

You're the one that I should kill. I'm finding no reason to keep you alive.

I followed behind Maxwell, not wanting to leave Emily on the bed.

A door creaked.

We both stopped and turned.

Luka walked in with huge bags of Chinese food from the basement entrance. He froze when he saw us.

"Don't worry," I said. "He's a friend."

Luka scowled at Maxwell, and then his gaze took in the dead men around him. "This day will never end. I'm ready to leave New York."

"Me too," I said. "I am going next door to see the footage of Rumi's murder."

Luka's jaw clenched.

"I'll be fine." I patted my friend's back. "Watch Emily. But make sure you eat, clear the bodies, and make sure there's food leftover for Emily."

The big man nodded.

Maxwell muttered under his breath as he walked off to the front door, "And make sure Emily doesn't wake up and kill you."

I grinned, when he opened the door for me.

"You think that's funny?" Maxwell watched as I walked through the doorway.

"It's definitely an appealing character flaw for a woman. At least for a man like me."

Maxwell led me out to the hallway. "I would rather have a chick with big tits verses her being a serial killer."

I scrunched my face in confusion. "Serial killer?"

"Emily." Chuckling, Maxwell walked over to his door, stopped, and unlocked it with a key. "Oh. . .you haven't been paying attention, have you?"

Chapter 18
Maxwell

Why did Emily tell him? I don't get it.

Emily never talked about shit like that. I couldn't figure out why she would decide to confess it to the Russian of all people.

But, that's not the only bad news. There's more.

The Russian had sex with Emily.

I didn't know if that would be a good or bad thing. Usually when guys slept with Emily, they wanted to do it again. So much that they stalked and tried to find ways to possess her. Sneaking into her place while she was sleeping. Creepy shit. Forcing her to work for them in some way that made her feel like she was in a bird cage.

Sometimes she killed them.

Other times I killed them without her knowing. How could I not? Since breaking me out of that boys' home years ago, Emily had taken care of me. I've never gone hungry or homeless with her. She always provided and made sure I was good to go.

What will this one do? What will we have to do?

I'd never had the pleasure of making love to Emily. I couldn't help biology. I was the mirror image of my father. Thank God he'd been a good-looking man, sadly he was also a pedophile. He never touched me, but I'd later learned the truth from Emily and Kennedy.

Who knew if he bothered Xavier's daughters too? He always loved to play hide and seek with us, always finding the girls first. He never caught Darryl and me. Emily usually outsmarted him many times, hiding better than us all.

And then one day he found her, and she didn't want to play with him anymore.

But our families pushed it on her again and again, anytime there was a cookout or Sunday card game. And something twisted in her head. And the day she killed my father, she was never the same. Our lives changed. Their father died in the fire. Xavier's girls burned alive.

Emily went real dark after that, always playing with knives and screaming in the middle of the night. Xavier had us for three months.

We must've been the shittiest kids to have while he mourned. I fought kids all the time in school. Darryl stole anything around him, whether he wanted it or not. Emily just played with knives and hid in tunnels, making us all feel like scared cats. He had to come up to our school every other day due to one of us getting in trouble.

Social services took us from Xavier. They didn't believe he could take care of us, especially after the sketchy way his daughters had died in the basement fire.

They kept Darryl and Emily together because they were siblings and then threw me in a boys' home. I grew suicidal, always having to be watched by a counselor. Emily damn sure didn't get better. It was just her luck that the foster home she landed in had adults with touchy fingers.

By the second foster home, she'd run away with Darryl. They found me in a boys' home and freed me.

And we never were caged again, running through the concrete jungles of New York, roaring and climbing. Hiding in sewers. Sleeping in libraries. Stealing our food from fruit and vegetable stands. Pick pocketing tourists in Times Square. Smoking thrown out cigarette butts. Living in the wild within skyscraper forests and brick valleys.

Does this guy understand that she won't be trapped, not by anyone? And that where she went, I did too, never leaving her side, never letting anyone get too close to her?

The door shut behind us.

The Russian turned to me.

Why does Emily always fuck the big, scary guys? It's going to be a bitch killing this one.

"How much do you want to know?" I asked.

She's already told him secrets. Maybe, I could scare him away with the rest.

The accent was so deep, I almost didn't understand him as he said, "Tell me everything."

I snorted. "We'll have to go in here. My dad's old bedroom. It's the only place where I can guarantee Emily wouldn't go snooping in. Not that she would snoop."

I opened the bedroom door and turned on the light.

Eight photos of men decorated the back wall. News clipping were thumbtacked under the images. A map covered the other wall with multicolored thumbtacks for spots in Harlem.

Leaning against the wall, I let the Russian drink it all in.

Smart as he was, he said nothing, walking slowly inside, reading a few lines of each article, and then going on to the next one. One by one, he went through the stuff that I'd cut out and put on the wall. It lasted for a good ten minutes.

At the last image, he turned to me. "Emily is the Tinder Killer?"

"Yes."

A neutral expression covered his face. He walked over to the table by the window where I'd scored a few of the victims' criminal records.

He opened a few and flipped through the pages. "They were all suspected of rape. Did she know this before finding and killing them?"

"I don't think so. She never remembers, and we've never talked about this." I rose from the wall. "I found her in her bedroom one night covered in blood. She was just sleeping there with a knife in her hand. I called Xavier."

"The man that lives in the abandoned bus?"

Damn. Emily did you give him your social security number too?

"Yes," I said.

"He's like her uncle?"

"Yes." I sighed uncomfortable with him knowing so much. "Xavier called Darryl. We all decided not to tell her. We washed and dressed her. Cleaned her bedroom—"

"But you had no idea what she'd done?"

"No. Xavier only found that she'd messaged some guy on Tinder to hook up. We had the meet up address."

"Where was it?"

"A hotel. We had his picture from his Tinder account—D.t.f.Beast-Boy."

The Russian quirked his eyebrow at the name.

I continued, "I was going to check on Mr. Beast Boy the next day. But that morning, the hotel's maid found him. His face was all over the news. We matched it to his tinder account from her messaging."

I marked my neck. "She'd sliced dude deep, right here and then a long side swipe."

I carved a large cross on my chest with an imaginary knife. "Then she did a holy cross, crucifying him as Xavier would say. He's religious, when it comes to death."

Then I did a show of stabbing my groin. "And finally, she cut his dick off over and over."

The Russian swallowed.

Yeah. You're not grinning anymore, are you?

"After we found that out, Xavier gave her a heart locket for her birthday and said some bullshit about him always wanting to be with her."

"The locket tracked her?" he asked.

"Exactly. When she went on the move for her Tinder meets, one of us went to check it out."

"How many times does she meet with people?"

"Every other week. It's always a different person. But what we realized is that she didn't kill them all." I gestured to the pictures. "Just these eight."

"Men who had backgrounds of rape." He leaned his head to the side. "Do you think they tried to rape her?"

"I don't know. Xavier made us promise to keep it from her. He doesn't think her mind can handle it. She's smart, maybe a genius in some ways, but still fragile in many other ways. He wants to keep her safe."

The Russian nodded. "So, you three watched her, and when she killed someone, you cleaned it up?"

"Yes." I sighed. "The night Rumi died, Darryl was supposed to be watching her. He had Xavier's tracker. The next thing I know, he's waking me up in the middle of the night and saying that she killed Rumi."

"Rumi was on Tinder?"

"No." I walked out of the room, pulled the disk out of my pocket, and went to my laptop.

The Russian stuck his hands into his pockets and stalked over to me. His eyebrows furrowed, but other than that, he gave me no impression of what he was thinking.

It took a few minutes to turn on the computer and upload the footage. I'd seen it last night which was the reason I'd decided to get rid of the hooker.

"When I showed up to Rumi's that night, Darryl kept making sure that I was going to destroy the footage. He didn't press the matter, but it was clear he didn't want me to look at the recording." I pressed on the link to start the video. "I knew something was wrong and saved it. I just didn't know why he was so anxious about it, until I saw it today. He'd sounded off, when we talked on the phone."

"You've talked to him?"

"Yes. He said the Russians freed him."

He smiled and said to himself, "They're definitely working together."

"Who?" I asked.

"My step brother and Darryl."

And then puzzle pieces began to form in my head, giving me the whole picture. "Now, everything is making more sense."

The footage began to play.

We watched.

On my laptop, the image of Rumi's office appeared on the screen. A door opened. Darryl walked in, holding a very drunk Emily. She stumbled along with him, giggling and playing an imaginary flute or something with her hand.

"What did Darryl give her?" the Russian asked.

"Something more than liquor, for sure," I said.

Darryl left Emily on the leather love seat next to the office's window. They talked about something, but we couldn't hear the conversation. There were no voices with the recording. Eventually, Emily fell asleep, smiling and leaning her head on her brother's shoulder.

After a few minutes, he pulled out a knife, rose from the couch, laid her down, and placed the knife in her hand.

I gripped my desk hard, hating Darryl. "I don't know, if I could watch this for a second time."

"We'll have to show this to Emily." The Russian clenched his jaw. "No more secrets from her. She should know what she's capable of, and what she's done, or it won't ever stop."

"Good." I gave him a sad smile. "You can be the one to tell her."

"I will."

On the laptop, Darryl walked away from a sleeping Emily as she gripped a knife, he turned the light off.

"I have other cameras footage, but it just shows him leaving the condo. The security guard was knocked out from whatever Darryl gave him."

"Who killed the guard?"

"I did." I shrugged. "Sorry about that, by the way."

He waved it away. "You did it to protect her. If not, then she wouldn't have been around to protect me."

We returned to the screen.

I pressed a button to fast forward. "She'd been in the office, sleeping for a good two hours."

I stopped the fast forwarding. "Rumi shows up right here."

I paused and turned to the Russian. "Rumi was expecting a hooker in his office."

"She's missing now. Do you know about that?"

"Maybe."

He didn't ask further, and I didn't offer any new information.

I pressed play.

Rumi walked in and pressed the light. It didn't come on.

"Darryl must've turned off the electricity in that room with a breaker," I said.

Rumi knew someone was on the couch. Moonlight bathed that area as Emily snuggled on her side. Rumi peeled away his pants and rubbed himself as he waddled over to her.

"No. I can't watch this again." I walked off. "Basically, Rumi tries to have sex with Emily while she's sleeping."

"And she slices him." The Russian watched. "Side-swipe to the neck. The holy cross on his chest."

And then the Russian flinched for a second as he saw her signature move. "And then she cuts off his penis."

The Russian pressed the button to stop the footage. "She passed out after that?"

"Yes. Covered in blood. And when I got there and saw it all…I did something I shouldn't have."

"What?"

"I called Kennedy to help us. Darryl just had to carry Emily through the tunnel under Rumi's building. Kennedy would meet him in her office. She cleaned Emily up and got her ready for the showing the next night, leaving her in her office to sleep." I held out my hands. "Kennedy didn't know anything about it being Rumi or what Emily had done. We just told her that some shit had went down and she didn't need to know anything more."

"But someone figured Kennedy knew. Probably my step brother."

"Yes. Darryl wouldn't have killed Kennedy, but he wouldn't have stopped anyone else from doing it either."

"My brother was the one to commission Emily to paint the lions. Did Kennedy have anything to do with it?"

"Yes, she didn't get involved in the crime side too much. Kennedy loved the art business angle. She handled the whole commission."

"Then, it was definitely my brother." The Russian sighed and walked off. "You'll need to pack."

"Me?" I touched my chest. "Why?"

"We're going to Russia, but first we'll stop in Prague."

I held my hands out. "Say what now?"

"Pack for the cold, Maxwell. I'm sure it's snowing—"

"Listen—"

"No." The Russian appeared calm, but there was an edge in his voice. "I don't listen, and I'm usually not nice, but today I will be. You're invited to come along. Call it an adventure. Emily will be with me, and I have a feeling you'll want to be with her too. Perhaps, you can invite your Uncle. After what I've heard, he might want a vacation."

A vacation to Prague and Russia?

I raised my hands in the air. "Look. Emily wouldn't go to Russia. She's never even left New York."

"She's going." Rage blazed in his eyes. "Pack."

The Russian left me there with my hands up and an expression of shock on my face.

Chapter 19

Kazimir

Back at Emily's place, I caught Luka up on everything.

The big man had stuffed himself with several cartons of chicken fried rice. Grease smeared his chin. The dead bodies remained on the floor.

"Clean this up." I scowled. "Did you leave any food for Emily?"

"Yes. It's in the fridge."

I pulled out my phone, turned it on, and dialed a number.

My sister Valentina's voice came on. "Kazimir? Is that you?"

"Yes."

"They said you were dead!" Valentina screamed.

"I'm not."

"But—"

"Come pick me up, please." I turned the speaker option off and held the phone to my ear. "Tell no one, dear sister."

"Where are you?" she asked.

"Harlem."

Her voice shrieked. "New York?"

"Yes."

"Well. . .good."

"Bring our cousins."

"It will be that type of emergency?"

"Perhaps, everyone believes I'm dead. Let's let the murderer have a few days to enjoy himself."

And edge cut through her voice. "And who is the murderer?"

"Our sweet step brother."

She cursed under her breath. "I told you not to go by yourself with him."

"That's why I wanted to go. I needed to see."

"And you saw?"

"Yes. Now, I need to hop on a plane without anyone noticing. Yours will do. No one will think oddly of you coming to New York to see what really happened."

She chuckled on the other line. "You're correct. In fact, I'm already here. I arrived an hour ago from Toronto. Our cousins are with me."

"And where is little Natalya?"

"Safe." Worry laced her words. "But, we have more to discuss than your niece. Sasha is expecting me at dinner this evening. Do I go?"

"Yes. Keep your men with you. Be careful and get my painting. It's in the bedroom where my belongings are."

"What painting?"

"A lion trapped in a net with a mouse chewing away at the rope."

"Why? What's in the painting?"

"It's priceless. Do it for me."

She let out an exasperated breath. "What are we going to do, Kazimir?"

"That is for another day. Spend the night here. Talk to our lovely step brother Sasha. Don't tell him anything. I'll give you the address. Come later. I want to leave in the morning."

"And where will I tell the pilot to go?"

"Prague."

She made an aggravated noise. "But, I love New York. Can't we kill Sasha here? We've finally got the proof that he's a spineless traitor."

"No. We kill him back home. It'll be less of a National Incident. And when you come, bring me some clothes. You know what I like." I tried to finish the call, but she yelled at me for not calling her immediately. I listened for several minutes. She was my sister after all.

How could I explain that I'd been a part of a little mystery involving a woman that had absolutely caught my attention? Emily was a woman of many faces and lives. Just when I thought I knew her, she pulled a layer off and showed me something else.

"There will be friends coming with me," I said.

"Who?"

"Just make sure you're nice."

"Hmmm. Must be a woman."

"I will see you later."

I hung up, not willing to tell her more about Emily.

Luka stared at me as I placed my phone in my pants.

"What?" I asked my long time friend.

"Emily is coming with us?" Luka asked.

"Yes."

He stuffed his mouth with more rice and said nothing else.

In Emily's bedroom, I watched her sleep for a few minutes.

Life hasn't been fair to you, mysh. Don't worry. I'll change that.

I undressed and showered in her bathroom. I hadn't cleaned up since fucking her on the desk. I still wore her scent like cologne and didn't really want to wash it away.

That's okay. I'll have her perfume on me again.

I finished, toweled, and didn't even wonder what I would wear. My sister was a mischievous creature. She'd be here earlier than I'd asked with more clothes and other things than I needed.

I kept the towel wrapped around my waist as I lay down next to Emily and gazed up at the ceiling.

Darryl told Sasha that his sister killed men. I'm sure of it. Darryl couldn't kill Rumi himself, but he knew his sister would in the right situation.

I added Emily's brother to my list of future dead people. Granted, we were all future dead people, but Darryl and Sasha's time would come earlier than they'd expected.

Emily killed Rumi. After carrying her back to her gallery, Darryl returned to the apartment to be a witness. Maxwell cleaned everything up, confused me with new cuts on the corpse and the sick stuff with the intestines. Later, I arrived to torture Darryl.

"We don't need to kill this guy," Sasha had said when we were heading to Rumi's building. *"Keep him alive."*

Sasha had turned away while I tortured Darryl. I'd figured it was the blood, but it was because they were friends.

Sasha had lit his cigarette, inhaled, and blew out a circle. "Maybe, we should ask him questions. Instead of choke him."

And then Darryl pointed me to Emily. It all worked out perfectly for them. Once I entered the gallery and spotted the paintings of lions, I was intrigued. Sasha had used my own spiritual logic on me.

In the limo, he'd chuckled. "Carl Jung is dead, and you will be too, if you don't stop with your meaningful coincidences."

"There's no such thing as a coincidence, my friend. It's all connected." I'd tapped the side of my head. *"That's what keeps us ahead of everyone else. I keep my eyes open."*

"You keep your eyes open? That's why?" Sasha had laughed. *"Maybe, we're also ahead of everyone else, because you don't mind peeling the skin off men one strip at a time, when they betray you."*

"Loyalty keeps us strong."

"I agree, so leave your dead man and his meaningful coincidences alone, as well as this mouse."

But in the end, I held on closer to the mouse, and Emily was what saved me.

Meaningful coincidences do matter, Sasha. Even if you triggered the first few with your commission of lion paintings.

Once I saw Emily, she'd trapped my attention. I hadn't known it at the time, but she'd cornered my interests. My cock knew we were going to fuck her, before my mind did.

Sasha probably laughed as I went on and on about the lions and her paintings.

I had smiled. "Mysh. That's what I will call her. My little mouse."

Sasha had laughed. "I think you're just looking for an excuse to fuck her."

"I don't need to create one. She's beautiful and smart. That's enough."

"Well, she's not for fucking. . ."

He'd said that, knowing that I would continue to pursue her. It was written all over the universe, whether he'd commissioned the paintings or not.

We were supposed to meet.

And the proof was in the magic that arose, when we united together. Not even a bomb could destroy us. What Sasha hadn't bet on was how resourceful and smart Emily was.

So, what did Darryl and Sasha think would happen?

Either Emily would kill me, as she murdered most men. And then my people would kill her. Or we both would die in the bomb the next day. Either way, the problem would be solved.

Darryl wouldn't have to spend some nights cleaning up his sister's serial killer mess. He probably figured that she deserved to die, that she was a monster.

She's no monster. She's just been fighting by herself too long. I'll stop the fighting, and then let's see if she'll have to kill anyone again.

On the bed, Emily groaned as she rolled over to me. She opened her eyes and widened them.

I made no movement, finally understanding that Emily was not the type of woman you woke from sleep.

I'm glad she doesn't have a knife around.

She scanned the space, glancing from side to side, and then letting her gaze fall on my damp, bare chest and then my towel. "What. . ."

She sat up and gripped a knife in her hand, letting it rest in her lap.

I edged back. "Where the hell did you get that knife? You didn't have one."

She parted her lips and dropped it on the center of the bed. "There are a bunch of knives taped to the head board. I always grab one, when I wake up. It's the first thing I do, before opening my eyes."

We'll have to change that.

"What do you remember?" I asked.

She blinked and then rubbed her eyes. "I. . .no. . .that can't be right. Max said I killed Rumi."

"You did." I couldn't sugar coat this anymore. My sister would be here soon, and we'd have to head away from this state. Sadly, this part of my plan needed to be rushed.

"I. . .killed him?" she asked.

"Yes. Maxwell had the footage. I watched it in his apartment."

She got up from the bed. "Wait a minute. How long have I been out?""

"Almost two hours."

"Fuck." She hugged herself. "That long?"

"You've done this before."

"But, not for that long." She put her back to me.

"Yes, Emily, you've done this before."

She turned to me. "What?"

"I have to rush this. You deserve time to understand this." I walked over to her and gently grabbed her hands. "Maxwell cleaned up Rumi after you killed him. Your brother brought you to Rumi's office to do it."

Her bottom lip quivered. "Darryl knew I would kill him?"

"Yes, because Maxwell and he have cleaned up your other messes."

She closed her eyes and whispered to herself. "So, then those aren't just nightmares."

"You have dreams of killing people?"

"Sometimes."

I pulled her into me.

She trembled against my chest. "What else?"

I had to tell her even though I didn't want to. "You're the Tinder Killer."

Her legs gave out, but she didn't pass out.

I helped her regain balance. "No, Emily. Stay with me."

"No. No. That's not true." She backed away. "I'm not going to let you all tell me who I am—"

"There's lots of proof."

"Where?"

"In Maxwell's apartment."

She covered her mouth with both hands. "No. That's crazy. There's no way. . ."

"I have a proposition for you."

She looked at me but didn't say anything.

"I need you to do more than wash for me."

Her bottom lip quivered. "What?"

What do I need her to do?

I still hadn't figured it out myself. I just knew that she couldn't leave my sight. That our story wouldn't end here in Harlem with me going and her staying here.

"I'll tell you more, once we get to Russia."

She inched back. Her voice screeched. "Russia?"

"My sister's going to give us a ride."

She swallowed. "I can't go—"

"You don't have much of a choice, Emily. Your picture is on every television screen in New York, probably even more than that. If they find out you're alive, they'll come asking questions. If Sasha knows you're alive, he'll kill you. And I won't be here to save you—"

"He would have to catch me first."

I smiled. "No, I won't risk it."

"I've. . ." She shook her head. "I've never left Harlem. I've never even been on a plane."

"Then, you're lucky. You'll be going in style. My sister's plane is even bigger than mine and dripping with luxury."

She ran her fingers through her hair. "I can't go—"

"Maxwell and your Uncle are going."

"They are not."

"They are, and you are too." I closed the distance between us. "The police will figure out that you are the Tinder Killer. With Sasha and your brother on your tail, someone will squash you."

Her chest rose and fell like she'd been running.

"But, I won't let that happen, Emily. No one will ever touch you, unless you want them to. No one will ever harm or violate you, lie or deceive you. No one." I wrapped my arms around her. "You'll work for me."

She leaned her head against my chest as if accepting defeat. "And is that all I will be doing for you. . .working?"

"I'm not stupid enough to think that I can put you on a leash, Emily. You'll be free in Russia."

In some ways. . .

She blew out a long breath. "I don't know, Kaz."

I grinned at the nicknamed she gave me. "Trust me, Emily. Just like I trusted you in the tunnels. Let me guide you to safety."

Sighing again, she looked up at me. "Okay. I want to use one of my two favors."

Surprised, I said, "Go ahead."

"Hold my hand, while we're on the plane. At least some of the time."

I chuckled. "I'll let you keep your two favors still. I already planned on doing that."

She stepped out of my arms and I pulled her back to me.

"I promise to protect you." I nipped at her lips.

Shaking her head, she backed away, never letting me catch her again.

"Then, I will use my other favor."

I raised my eyebrows. "What do you want?"

"We don't have sex anymore, not if I'm going to work for you. . .and even if I wasn't working for you. I just like. . .one-time flings, nothing more."

"One-time?" I winked at her. "I would rather you say *one more time*."

She stirred in front of me.

"With this new knowledge, I'm sure you're anxious and confused." I licked my lips. "I'm sure you need someone to take the edge off. And trust me, when I say this. . ." The rest of my words held a razor sharped edge. "You are no longer allowed to use Tinder."

She widened her eyes.

"You get in too much trouble with it, and you'll be busy." I adjusted my towel, walked back to her bed, and lay down. "If you don't want to fuck anymore, little *mysh*, that's fine. Your body is not why I'm bringing you to Russia."

At least, it isn't the only reason.

She slowly walked to the edge of the bed and stared down at me. "So. . .you understand?"

"Yes. You don't want to fuck anymore." My cock got hard under the thin towel.

It hadn't been lost on me that she kept letting her gaze drop to the hump.

How long will you deny yourself?

I tried to keep the desire out of my voice. "Are you hungry?"

"Yes."

"Luka brought food. It's in the kitchen."

She blinked. "Oh."

I smirked. "You thought I was talking about something else."

Annoyance crept at the corner of her eyes.

"You must be anxious and edgy, Emily."

She shook her head at me.

I rubbed my cock over the towel. "As I've said before, I'm here for you, but I won't take you. I've heard a bloody rumor that you can't be taken."

She watched me slide my hands down my length and then squeeze the tip hard.

She'd done this to me, made me fucking crazy around her. If she thought we would never have sex again, then she'd banged her head, when she'd passed out. I would have her in Harlem, in Prague, and Russia too. And I wouldn't share her with anyone else.

But most of all, I will let her figure that out all on her own.

I licked my lips.

Her breath hitched in her throat.

"Oh, Emily. I wonder, if you would be open to some sort of compromise."

She squeezed her thighs together as she stood by the edge of the bed. "Compromise?"

"Maybe, we fuck one more time. Just once more. What could it hurt?"

She averted her eyes.

"We're good friends. We trust each other. Our relationship has grown from the very desire to save each other's lives. Who else should help you knock the edge off, but me?"

A smile broke across her face.

"Hmmm. I love, when you smile."

"Most men would've run, after all the things you've heard about me. I'm a fucking serial killer—"

"Don't think about it."

"Most men would run."

"Do I look like a man that runs?"

Her nipples hardened poking the front of her shirt.

I grunted. "Come here."

Chapter 20
Emily

What did one do when the most powerful man in the world told them to come?

They came.

And that was what I did, but first I slipped off my jeans and shirt. I wore a new bra and panty set underneath. I hadn't planned on having sex with him again, but still I'd picked the sexier items to wear before taking them back into the tunnels.

The bra and panties were all crimson lace. They hid nothing from him. He could see the outline of my nipples and the space between my thighs.

He directed his gaze down my body from my head to my toes, curving his lips into a wicked smile.

"Why do you want me to come to you?"

"Oh Emily, do you know how dangerous you are?"

"No." I touched the straps on my shoulders but didn't move them.

His words were a growl. "Come here."

My eyes drooped with lust.

"I want to undress you," he whispered. "I want to slip that lace off your body."

I shouldn't have, but I crawled to him, needing to forget yet again. He'd told me that I killed people. I didn't want to believe him, but deep inside of me I knew there was some truth to it.

But I couldn't think about it. I refused to. I'd killed before. Death had been around me since I was ten. Tragedy came and went. Twists always hit and knocked me down, but I never stayed on the ground.

I always jumped back up.

I'm not what they said I am. I won't think about it.

My chest ached, and I shut the thoughts away into a mental room where I kept tons and tons of other stuff. Other moments I never wanted to deal with again.

In front of me lay a powerful man, dripping in masculine gorgeousness.

And I would fuck him. I would ride his cock until I forgot about Darryl's deceit, Maxwell's secrets, and Kazimir's new position for me.

Am I really going to Russia? No way. I'll get out of it somehow.

Everything could wait.

And so, I crawled to Kazimir, so horny my skin burned with hunger.

On all fours, I moved toward him. His gaze went to my cleavage. I crawled over his taut legs and muscular thighs. The towel still wrapped around him, but his cock had tented the front, hiking the center up.

I rubbed my body against his cock's tip as I continued to journey up his beautiful body—all curved and hard. Sculpted tanned skin. Tight and smooth. Perfect, except for the scars that marred his side.

Still on all fours, I hovered over him. My face was barely two inches from his. Our noses almost touched.

"You've been shot?" I asked.

"Of course. You don't get to where I am without being shot a few times."

"Hmmm." I lowered a little and kissed his lips. Before he could capture my tongue, I lifted back up. "If I go to Russia with you, will you promise not to get shot anymore?"

"I can't promise that, but I've been really good at avoiding it." He raised his head to me and sucked on my bottom lip.

I pulled in my breath as he reached out to me, the tips of his fingers tenderly grazing my chin. Heat spread out from his touch, flooding my senses.

He moved his hands down my body and gripped my hips, pulling my body against his. "I like how you said the word *if.*"

"I did."

He slid his hands over my ass and squeezed. The whole time he rubbed his cock against my center. "Don't think that because you're half-naked and on top of me, that you'll be able to do what you want to do."

"I—"

He flipped me onto my back. "You're coming to Russia. If you stayed, I would envy the NY winds that got to touch you, when I couldn't. I'd be jealousy of this country because it had you far away from me."

My heart hammered in my chest.

"And you'll love my country." Inch by inch, he lowered to my breast, landing kisses along the border of my bra. "We're going to have fun."

"What's fun to you?"

He gripped the front clasp of my bra between his teeth and ripped it away.

I shrieked.

The material continued to rip from me. I moved my arms out of the straps, so he wouldn't rip me away with him. He spat the bra out on the bed. "I have so many plans for you, Emily."

I could've orgasmed just from the sound of his voice. It was that sexy. After hearing everything, I couldn't deal with any slow burn foreplay. I needed him now. Hard and fast. His cock inside of me, pumping fast and deep into me.

I yanked away the stupid towel. His cock flopped out, bumping against my stomach. I shuddered, close to begging him to tear off my panties too.

"I love, when you look so greedy." He devoured my mouth.

I lapped at his tongue.

Groaning, he tore his mouth away from my mine and reached for my night stand's drawer. "I assume there are condoms in here."

"There are."

He yanked it opened and frowned. "More boxes and knives."

"You can never have enough condoms and knives."

Silent, he ripped the foil on the packet with one hand and his teeth, hovering over me. That strong build scared me. But in a way his hugeness comforted me too, I knew he wouldn't hurt me. I felt it in my gut.

I promise to protect you.

I let his words comfort me as I scooted out of my panties and slung them to the floor.

"What were you thinking about?" He slipped the condom along his thick length.

"I can't wait to have your cock inside of me."

"That wasn't an answer," He licked his lips. "But, I'll take it this time."

I smirked.

He moved his hands down my body, caressing each inch. "You won't need so many boxes of condoms in Russia."

So naughty, I couldn't help it. "I'll take some just in case. I'm starting to like Russian men."

His expression went neutral.

Okay. Sorry. Maybe, that wasn't funny.

"Really?" He shoved my legs wide apart to further accommodate his hips. "Tell me more about this attraction."

"I didn't know Russian men could be so big." I raised my hand to hold his cock.

He knocked it away. "Hmmm."

I pouted. "What was that for?"

He lowered a little, teasing me and touching the tip of his cock to my opening. Writhing under him, I craned my neck forward to watch the erotic torture more.

"Please," I whispered.

"No one else can be in your bed, Emily." He pushed in that first delicious inch. The thick head of his sex pulsed, hard and demanding.

I gripped the sheets and arched forward. "More. . .please."

"You know what you're doing to me, Emily." He pierced me with another inch of his cock. The mushroom tip disappeared into my pussy. "But, do you know what I'm doing to you?"

Another inch.

I cried out in lust.

"Oh, Emily." He dove deep into me. The air punched hard out of my lungs. I was full with him.

I fell back into the bed, rocking with his rhythm.

"It already feels like it's been too long since I fucked you." Shifting his pumping to slowly and dominating, he slipped inside of me and pulled out, working his thick abs against my clit, slowly. So painstakingly slow. Our bodies lovingly molded against the other. Hard muscle against soft flesh. Rough inhales between soft exhales.

I clenched around him, my sex sucking him. So hungry. Greedy. Starving for more of him.

Slowly, he pulled all the way out of me.

My pussy went empty. Shock hit me.

I panted. "Kaz?"

He raised his eyebrows at me. Lust blazed in his eyes. "We can have sex only one more time?"

I bit my lip.

"Answer me."

I widened my eyes. "Maybe another time."

He gazed at me under hooded eyes. "Maybe?"

"Please, come back to me."

"What do you want, Emily?"

"Your fat cock inside of me."

He kissed me.

I tore away from his lips. "Now."

Growling, he licked the curve of my neck.

I trembled and wrapped my arms around his neck as if I could pull him down and inside of me.

"Only one more time?" he whispered against my throat and then nibbled the curve.

"Definitely another time, Kaz, please."

He landed a soft kiss on my lips and whispered, "And another?"

"Yes."

He dove back into my pussy, catching me by surprise. "And another and another."

"Yes," I moaned.

So deep and smooth. Every delicious movement. And his muscles flexed as he pumped. And he drove me crazy. Gorgeous and hypnotizing. So much power radiated from him. And he was a wild beast. Not controlled by anyone or anything.

Gripping my hips with those large hands, he drove into me, again and again, his thrusts rough to the point of brutal.

I needed this.

All my problems disappeared. Everything vanished away. All I had to think about was him and how good he made me feel. He fucked me the rest of the night. Even after I came. He wouldn't stop. It was mindless abandon. Pumping and pounding. Fast and then slow. Hard and then soft.

The second time, I came harder than ever before.

"Y*a lyublyu trakhat' tebya*," he whispered, holding me firmly in his hands, lovingly punishing my sex. He gave me no time to catch my breath. He pushed me more. Thrusting and pumping. My breaths were strangled gasps.

"Kaz." I shut my eyes and let my head fall back. I didn't know what else he could want from me, but I was willing to give it.

And when I came the third time, he finally orgasmed with me.

And we tore into shattered bits of who we'd been before ever meeting each other. I knew I would never be the same again. Too much had moved between us. Too much had changed, and a lot of it happened right in my bed.

"*Ty mne nuzhen.*" He drove into my pussy and froze, planting himself inside of me, balls deep. Tremors of pleasure rode me. A delirious fog filled my head. I had no thoughts or concerns. Just his face in front of mine—caught in complete pleasure.

He dropped his forehead to my shoulder. Grunting, he drew back and then plunged deeper again.

"Jesus, Kaz." I clutched his strong back.

He lifted my hips to meet another hard thrust.

"Fuck," he murmured under his breath. His cock jerked inside of me.

"Oh God," I mumbled, unable to feel any more pleasure. My pussy had went numb.

"*Ty takoy khoroshiy,*" he groaned again and lifted his head to stare at me.

And I drank the beauty of him as he finished coming. The danger left his eyes. He gripped my hips harder and groaned deeper, freezing us right there, not letting his cock move one inch. So beautiful to watch, he slipped away and moaned so loud, a hot shiver sliced up my spine.

We collapsed on the bed.

He moved to my side.

I remained on my back, finally catching my breaths. Exhausted, all I could do was gaze at the ceiling.

"My step brother is smart," Kazimir whispered between hurried breaths as he rested on his back. "You just might kill me."

Panting, I scooted to him and lay on his chest. "What did all of those Russian words mean?"

Closing his eyes, he smiled. "They are words that I've never said before."

"But, what did you say?"

"One day, I'll tell you them in English."

I fake pouted. "Then, I should learn Russian."

"You should. You'll be living there."

"Temporary."

He caressed my back.

"Could you teach me some Russian?" I asked.

"Of course."

"What do you want to know?"

"Hit me with something cool."

He opened his eyes and stared at me. Something new lingered in his gaze—a warmth I'd never seen in them. The first night I'd met him, they'd been so cold and deadly. Now this all-consuming warmth filled his pupils.

He whispered in that sexy accent, "*Shob tebe deti v sup srali.*"

I spent several seconds repeating it. He corrected me a few times. And then on my tenth try, he nodded. "Perfect."

I lifted my head and smiled at him. "*Shob tebe deti v sup srali.*"

"Exactly."

"Awesome. What does it mean?"

"I hope your kids shit in your soup."

Laughter fled from my mouth. My body rocked. I sat up in the bed. "Really? I wanted some good lines to get to know your country and people, and that's the phrase you chose."

"It's a good line."

"I need to know something that I'll be saying a lot to people."

"Trust me, Emily. You'll be telling a lot of people that you hope their children shit in their soup."

I shook my head. "*Shob tebe deti v sup srali.*"

He winked at me. "Good job, *mysh*."

Chapter 21

Maxwell

Someone shook me.

Yawning, I opened my eyes.

A blonde woman with liquid blue eyes stared back at me. "What size are you?"

"What the fuck?"

She backed away, allowing me to drink in more of her. She damn sure was a princess. Looked rich from head to toe. Everything was polished—nails and clothes, shoes and make-up. Flawless. Sexy. Stunning.

"Who are you?" I sat up in the bed. Emily's Russian wasn't there, but a bunch of other Russians were, including this woman standing by my bed.

Although she had a light voice, it was heavily laced with an accent. "You're sleeping beauty and I'm the princess that comes kisses you awake."

I cleared my throat. "What?"

She giggled. "You'll need clothes."

Another man held a gun and walked around as he scanned my bedroom. He gazed out of my window. "Mr. Maxwell, the plane will leave in two hours."

"Yes. Yes. But, he needs clothes." She pouted. "And the plane will leave, when I say."

"Who are you people?" I slipped my hand under my pillow and gripped my gun.

The man stopped and stared at the pillow that my hand was under. "I don't know what you're getting, but you should leave it alone. This is Valentina. Her brother Kazimir asked her to get you."

I continued to hold my gun. "For what?"

The man frowned as if I shouldn't even ask questions, but just do what I'm told. "We're going to be leaving in an hour."

I let go of the gun, sat up some more, and leaned my back against the headboard.

The Russian was serious about all of us leaving.

"You're *his* sister?" I asked.

She nodded. "Yes."

The big man with her grumbled, "Get up and get dressed. No more questions."

"Stop being mean, Oleg." She batted her eyes at him. "He's our friend." She turned back to me. "I've brought clothes, but I don't think I have your size." Valentina studied my arms and smiled. "You're not a Michael Kors's man. You're a Tom Ford man."

She continued on about what type of man I was, but I couldn't tell you a single word she'd said.

She pointed to Oleg. "Go to Barney's and get some more socks."

"Your brother wants me next to you at all—"

"Pretend I'm in Barney's with you."

"Valentina, that is not how—"

"Kazimir is right next door. How could I not be any safer?"

Oleg frowned. "I will send someone else to get them, Valentina."

The whole time they went back and forth, I was completely entranced by her mouth and her body. She moved constantly as she talked. Every few seconds, she made hand gestures to punctuate her speech. It made me smile as I thought about tying her hands to my headboard and making her beg me to fuck her. I would sink deep inside her sweet little Russian cunt, pounding into her.

Then, maybe she would reconsider storming into my bedroom and waking me up from a good sleep.

She returned to me and blinked her eyes. "Why are looking at me like that?"

"You're a beautiful woman in my bedroom." I'm wondering if you're going to kiss me."

She glanced over her shoulder. "Tell Tommy to get over here with some clothes."

The man on the right rolled his eyes. A knife had been tattooed through his neck with blood dripping red ink at the tip. "Valentina, we don't have time—"

"Call him!" she roared.

Silence filled the room. The man with the inked knife, pulled out his phone, and backed out of the room. Everyone returned their gazes to me.

"Wakey. Wakey." She clapped her hands and headed out of my room. "Take a shower so you can try on your new clothes."

"I don't need new clothes," I called back.

No response came.

Everyone else left.

An hour later, I was dressed in a designer suit—one that the crazy blonde had picked out. A tailor had finished the stiches right up to the minute Emily's Russian growled that it was time to leave. He wore a new suit too—sleek and polished from head to toe.

Somehow Emily had convinced Xavier to come with us. He'd dragged himself out of that abandoned bus, showered in my bathroom, and let the evil blonde wrap him in a red, blue, and white plaid ensemble. A white fur coat went down to his ankles. Xavier even had a cane that he enjoyed twirling.

He looks like a pimp.

Currently as we stood at the private gate of the airport, Xavier twirled the cane too close to me.

I turned to him. "Would you stop, X?"

He set the cane's bottom on the floor and tapped out a beat. "You've been grumpy the whole time."

"You don't think this shit is crazy? We're just jumping on a plane with this—"

"We were just cleaning up Emily's dead men weeks ago. This don't seem crazy to me. I'm actually glad we have some help on that."

"Help?" I snorted. "This Russian's not going to help her. He's going to use her."

"Don't look to the future, young one. You don't know what the future is going to bring." Xavier tapped his cane on the ground again. "Just two days ago you didn't know you would be here. Just stay in the moment. Keep your eyes open."

"Trust me. I am." I watched Emily and her Russian walk in, flanked by four huge men. They'd taken the limo behind us. More men marched behind them, my heart tightened. Usually, we all worked together. Emily never let any other group unite with us. It would just be the originals—Xavier, Kennedy, Darryl, her, and me. Now Russians surrounded us, and I wasn't quite sure if they were our friends.

I frowned. "Emily looks comfortable."

Xavier turned my way. "That's a good thing. She deserves some rest."

"She took the serial killer thing well."

"We know who we are, even when we don't admit it to ourselves." He tapped his chest. "You can never lie to your insides."

I sighed. "Are you going to be talking like some fucking ghetto sage the whole trip?"

"Yes. I'm feeling energized." He adjusted the fur on his shoulder. "This is my destiny. Now it's all making sense."

Emily scanned the space and spotted us.

Our gazes met.

She smiled.

My body warmed as I nodded.

She's still the same Emily.

She turned to Kazimir, whispered something, and then left him, heading over to Xavier and me. Her Russian didn't appear pleased at all from her absence. He gazed the whole time at her, as she walked away. Granted, the back of her must've been hard not to look at because surely the front had my cock hard.

"She looks good too." Xavier tapped a little beat on the floor with his cane. "Go on, Emily."

Black leather covered her whole body. Fitted pants, not tight, but damn sure not loose. A black leather jacket stopped high on her waist. It had a hood that was trimmed in white fur. For now, it hung on her shoulders.

The heels of her boots clicked toward us. And most of the men stopped the conversation they were involved in to glance her way.

She got to us and filled the space with this sweet perfumed scent.

I had so much to ask and even say to her, but all I could mumble was, "You smell good."

"Thanks." She touched my jacket. "You look damn good, Max."

"I try."

Her Russian watched us from across the lobby. The blonde talked to him and some other men, but his gaze remained on Emily and my exchange.

Fuck him. Get used to it. We rock together.

I looked down at her. "What are we doing, Emily? This is crazy."

"You have to trust me, Max. I'm still looking out for us. . .like you all looked out for me. Thank you for. . .all that." She blew out a long breath, got between Xavier and me, and leaned against the wall. "And being truthful, I really don't know what we're doing. But, what options do we have?"

Xavier chimed in, "Max said that Jamaicans ransacked your apartment last night."

"Yeah." She nodded. "Kaz and Max killed them. Luka got rid of their bodies."

"Kaz?" I gave her the side-eye.

She ignored me. "At first, I thought they were there to take my money under the boards, but after I got to see the... *whole picture*... Daryll must've known that I was still alive, due to the locket."

She pulled out the heart locket on her chest.

Xavier shook his head. "How could Darryl try to kill you?"

"He thinks I'm a monster."

"You're not." Xavier grabbed her hand.

She gave him a weak smile and moved her hands. "I am, but thanks. Whether those eight guys were rapists before or not, doesn't help me sleep better. Some of them were fathers and brothers—"

"Is that why you're running to Russia with *Kaz*?" I faced her.

"Yes, Max. That's why I'm running to Russia with *Kazimir*." She poked my chest with her finger. "Do you have something to say?"

"I don't get what's going on with you two." I admitted. "You're acting different."

"That's fair, Max." She shrugged. "I don't understand why I'm acting different either, but I feel good about my decisions. Do you trust me?"

"Always."

"We have to be together on this or it won't work out." She looked at me and then turned to Xavier. "Life has shown that we need each other. When we hit Russia, we stay together. No secrets between us three."

"Okay." I nodded.

"This is my vacation." Xavier twirled his cane. "Let's not go there and get in more trouble. Enjoy the new culture and people."

"This isn't a vacation, X." She glanced behind me. "Darryl has been working with Kazimir's brother Sasha on this whole plan for at least a year."

Xavier frowned. "That's after you started killing guys. How do you know your brother has been planning it for that long?"

"Because I got the secret commission to paint the lions a year ago, and it was his brother Sasha who did it."

My muscles tightened. "You mean to tell me that Darryl has been playing us for that long?"

"Yeah." She tapped her heart locket. "So, I hope he knows that I'm alive, and I hope he watches me go to Russia, and soon as I hit the ground, I'm breaking the locket."

"He won't know if you're alive or not. He might think someone has your locket. I've got a better idea." Xavier snatched the chain off her, walked away, and threw it in a janitor's cart. "I like him thinking you're dead. This way it'll go to a landfill."

"Fuck it." Emily grinned. "Meanwhile, we go to Russia and we face whatever we face together."

She stared at both of us. "We remain together. We have each other's backs, and most of all. . .we don't keep secrets from each other anymore. No matter how fucked up it could be. No matter how much it would tear up my mind."

Xavier beat me to the question. "Are you sure about that, Emily?"

"I'm sure." Her expression turned sad. "I don't like what I am, but I. . .just. . .just don't keep that stuff from me. And if I get too dangerous, then—"

"Shut up. We're not killing you." I wanted to hug her, but that wasn't our way. I doubted she could even deal with my hands on her. The few times I did hold her, she kept her eyes closed and never looked at me.

But none of it mattered.

Although I was always attracted to her—she did have breasts—I loved her more like a step sister. I couldn't live without her, but I knew there might be a time when we would have to separate.

I looked across at her Russian.

He continued to watch us as others conversated with him.

This one won't be going anywhere soon.

Some other men walked into the building.

Shit.

"Emily." I gestured to the newcomers. Most of them had bland khakis on and white shirts, but their blue wind jackets were the most important. On the side, three yellow letters decorated them—F. B. I.

"I'll be right back." Emily walked back over to the Russian.

The idiot hadn't even noticed the FBI walking in. His gaze remained on Emily, studying her hips as she returned to him.

Even more interesting, none of the Russian men appeared nervous about the FBI's presence either.

What's going on?

"Keep your eyes open, young one." Xavier twirled his cane. "Going off with this guy might be the best thing ever."

"What the fuck are you talking about?" I kept my voice low. "It looks like we won't even be getting on the plane."

Xavier twirled the cane some more.

A redhead walked in with a pencil skirt and white shirt. She wore a FBI jacket too. The other FBI guys gave her space as she headed straight to Emily and her Russian.

I glared at them. "I wish they would've let me bring my guns."

"You won't need your gun on this trip, but when we get to Russia. We'll figure it out."

"Why are you so calm right now?" I asked Xavier.

"Just be happy that you're not the smartest person in the room."

Chapter 22

Kazimir

Emily talked to Maxwell like any woman would talk to a close and loving friend. Still, tension built in my chest. It was crazy that I couldn't stop watching her.

Emily smiled at Maxwell, and my tension switched little anger. Her smiles were mine. Her every precious glance belonged to me too. She just didn't know that. Granted, I'd just realized it myself as I studied her next to him, not enjoying their closeness. However, I was smart and fully understood I could never control her.

I'll figure out this Maxwell thing. It shouldn't bother me that she's smiling at him. He's only been like a brother. He's only ever protected her. . .for me. He just didn't know it then.

I clenched my fists and gained control of myself. I wouldn't kill Maxwell, but he'd learn his place soon enough.

The FBI walked in next.

I'd expected them. Valentina stirred. My men turned to me for my order. Seconds later, Emily spotted the agents too. Her face filled with worry.

Little mysh, you still don't understand who I am? What's the FBI to a me?

Emily walked over. Every curve moved with lushness under her clothes. Soon, I would have them off and on the plane's floor. I planned to be deep inside of her as the plane rose to the sky.

She got to my side right as the agents crowded in front of me. "Is everything okay?"

I nodded.

FBI Chief Gloria Stein stood in front of me. "So, you're alive?"

"Clearly," I said.

Gloria turned to Emily. "And who is this?"

None of your business.

I smiled. "I'm leaving the country."

"I see." She gestured to my sister's large plane. "And you want permission to leave?"

"Is that what our relationship is?" I wagged my finger at her. "My asking for your permission?"

She frowned. "I want the locations of—"

"You'll get them, when my party and I are back in Russia."

"And how do we know that we can trust you?"

"You don't have a choice." I held Emily's hands. "And this conversation is longer than I planned."

Gloria looked at our locked hands and then back to me. "You're the one that called me here, Kazimir."

"I'm adding three people to my protection." I handed her the list with Emily, Maxwell, and Xavier's name. "If their names come up for anything under the FBI, you call me directly."

She opened the paper and then closed it. "Who are these people and what did they—?"

"Have a good afternoon, Gloria."

I guided Emily away. Everyone in our party followed. My sister had brought many of her people. Most were our cousins that had fought with us for years. And of course, we now had the Harlem Crew—a name that my sister had coined for Xavier, Maxwell, and Emily.

"They're so adorable." My sister had clapped her hands. "I'm so glad they're coming. I want to dress them up. Especially her."

I held my arms up for the tailor as he fitted me for the third jacket that morning. "Valentina, you're too excited. They're not pets or dolls."

"I know. I know."

I lowered my arms as the tailor finished measuring. "Don't bother them."

"How can I bother them? They're the Harlem Crew. They're family." Then she raised her eyebrows. "Are they family?"

"I'm still. . .reviewing them."

She crossed her arms across her chest. *"It's not like you to bring people along that you've just met."*

"Emily saved my life."

"And the other two men?" she asked.

"They've saved her life. . .many times which means they're friends of mine for now."

Her expression brightened. *"This Harlem Crew has a lot of spunk."*

"Just don't bother them."

She smiled at me. *"And what else does Emily mean to you?"*

"I've already explained."

"When I arrived, you were both in the bedroom together."

I chuckled. *"That is what a man and woman does sometimes, Valentina. They are inside of a bedroom together. I believe that's how you got Natalya."*

"Are you in love with Emily?"

I grinned. *"How can I be in love with someone that I've just met?"*

"Something is happening with you, brother. You're acting different."

"A lot has happened, but nothing's different"

I hadn't lied to my sister. In many ways I didn't feel different, yet I had to admit that I acted out of character. It wasn't like me to travel with any woman, especially in such a chaotic time.

"Are you in love with Emily?"

"How can I be in love with someone that I've just met?"

"Something is happening with you, brother. You're acting different."

Maybe my sister had a point. Still I wasn't ready to think about it. Granted, I'd never been so consumed by any woman before. I didn't even know the last time I really looked at a woman, when she didn't have my cock deep down her throat.

"A lot has happened, but nothing's different"

In fact, I probably did lie to Valentina, but I would never admit it to her or anyone else. Emily had called to me from the very beginning.

Perhaps, she was meant to be mine one day. Since a kid, I'd always had a talent for trapping mice.

This mouse won't be easy to catch.

New York was supposed to be about Rumi and a possible oncoming war. Instead, I'd. . .fallen into something. Lust. Obsession. Desire. I couldn't point to it, but I was deep into the shit of it. After having Emily, I yearned for her more than ever before. My need was beyond comprehension and hard to describe, but still it burned thick inside of my soul.

Emily pulled me out of my thoughts. "Do you fly a lot?"

"Always. . .at least, when I'm allowed in that country."

"I doubt you would let a little travel ban stop you."

I smiled. "This is true."

Emily and I walked out of the private gate exit and onto the airplane. The whole time I held her hand, unable to not touch her. With each step, her fingers shivered against mine.

"What's wrong?" I asked as we got to the stairs leading to Natalie's plane.

"I've never been on a plane before."

"You'll be with me the whole time."

Emily widened her eyes. "Will that be enough, when we're up in the air?"

"Well, if you're feeling edgy. I can definitely think of ways to knock the edge off."

"I hate that I admitted that to you." She blushed. "You'll never stop saying that."

"I just enjoy knocking the edge off."

She sighed. "Me too."

We climbed onto the plane.

I got in front to lead the way. She must've thought that we would sit in the main area with everyone else, but I had other plans.

The tailor had finally finished. The suit fit right and had a silky texture. My sister always knew how to save the day.

"Thank you for giving me a ride," I said to Valentina.

She walked around me, checking out my suit. "How can I say no, when you bought me the plane in the first place."

"It's still nice."

The plane had been a sore spot for everyone. It made most jealous, especially Sasha.

It's probably why he decided to kill me. Didn't I buy her the plane over a year ago?

When Valentina had announced her pregnancy and that she was carrying my first niece, I had to buy her a plane and make sure my niece and her had no excuse to not visit me in Russia.

The cost was ungodly—running around eighty million—but it was for Valentina after all. A Gulfstream G660. 20,000 cubic feet of luxury cabin space. Designer outfitted. Comfy leather chairs that reclined all the way back for sleep. Plush couches. Large windows to bring in plenty of natural light. Two televisions. Dining area. Two bathrooms. One had its own walk-in shower. The other was a private bathroom connected to a master suite with a large bed.

My sister finished her assessment of my suit and nodded at the tailor. "Thank you."

The man gathered his items. His helpers got the rest.

Minutes later, they exited from Emily's place.

I smoothed the front of my jacket. "I must also ask you for another favor, Valentina."

She quirked one eyebrow. "What, Kazimir?"

"I want your bedroom for the flight."

She smirked at me as if she knew a wicked secret. "And will your Emily be joining you in there?"

"Yes."

"Interesting. Did you know that I have cameras in the room? I'll have to get them shut off."

"No, just give me the tapes."

She shook her head. "You should be focused on Sasha—"

"Can I use your bedroom for the trip?"

"Of course, you can, Kazimir. Who would say no to you?" She sighed. "You're going to fall for this Emily, and then things will really get interesting. I've never seen you in love."

"You're getting too excited." I left her there, but muttered under my breath, "I just want to. . .explore her."

On the plane, I guided Emily forward. Rustling and movement sounded behind me. Everyone else was probably climbing on too.

Excitement covered Emily's face as she took in every luxurious detail. "This is. . .a stunning plane."

I squeezed her hand. "Not bad for your first flight?"

"Not bad at all."

I led her past the main cabin.

"Where are we going?" Emily asked.

"We'll be in my sister's bedroom. It's about ten hours to Prague. I assumed you would want to lay down and be comfortable." I opened the door to the bedroom.

She slowly walked in. "You also thought that since I would be super nervous about flying, I may need you to knock the edge off?"

"I did plan for that." I shut the door. "And you did promise me another and another time. How many *anothers* did we say?"

She blinked. "I don't remember. I was too busy coming over and over."

"Hmmm."

She didn't sit down on the bed.

Instead we stood in front of each other.

She turned her head to the right and spotted her painting leaning against the wall. "How did you get that back?"

"My sister met with Sasha last night for dinner. She went into my room and took the painting with her, probably telling Sasha that she wanted something to remind her of me."

A huge smile spread across Emily's face.

"What else is on your mind?"

She turned her attention away from the painting. Her expression went back to serious. "The FBI agent. Who is she?"

I was wondering, when you would ask.

"She's been trying to catch me for years, but as you can see, it's never worked out."

"Have you ever. . .had sex with her?"

Shocked, I shook my head. "What made you ask that?"

"The FBI agent looked annoyed that I was around you and that we were holding hands."

But were you jealous, little mysh?

"It doesn't matter what annoys her," I said. "She's been trying to catch me for ten years. I've become an obsession for her. I'm sure, when she heard I'd died, she had no idea what else she would do with her life."

Grinning, Emily said, "She did look happy to see you alive, but. . .and I know you may not want to tell me—"

"No, we keep no secrets between us. You and I will always know everything about the other."

Emily raised her eyebrows. "Are you working with the FBI?"

"In some ways. A large part of my *organization* deals with weapons. That would mean I have contacts with many people the FBI would love to grab."

"Terrorists?"

"Yes. Terrorism has ranked higher on the FBI's to-do list, surpassing international organized crime." I took off my jacket and set it on the chair. "And lucky for Mrs. Stein, I happen to dislike terrorists. There's so many more ways to spend your time."

"So, you've given the FBI some terrorists?" she asked.

"I have."

"Who?"

"The big ones."

"And so, they leave you alone, when you fly into America?"

"Yes, and they leave me alone with a lot of things." I stalked over to her. "But...*leaving me alone* is a nice term for the FBI and my situation. Mainly, they promise not to get in my way, and I try not to kill them, when they do."

"It sounds like a very tricky relationship."

"It is." I wrapped my arms around her waist and drew her to me. "It's like ours."

"How are we tricky, Kaz?"

I couldn't help, but growl from the nickname. "*Tol'ko vy mozhete pozvonit' mne, chto.*"

She blinked. "Damn it. What did you say? It sounded so sexy."

"I said that 'Only you can call me that.'"

She blushed. "Kaz?"

"Yes, *mysh*. Only you can call me Kaz." I kissed her, sucking on that bottom lip. "Only you can say it."

She leaned away from me. "But, how are we tricky?"

"I don't think either one of us knows what we're doing with the other."

"My excuse is that I have no experience with things like this. I don't mess with a guy more than once." She shrugged. "It's easy that way."

"Unfortunately, I won't be easy." My jaw clenched. "And I want it more than once."

"As you've shown...over and over." She licked her lips.

"This will be tricky."

Emily stepped away from my arms. "It doesn't have to be. We could establish rules and be careful."

"No. I would break the rules with you."

She bit her lip.

"Take off your clothes and lay down on the bed."

She swallowed.

"We'll be leaving soon, and this is your first flight. I want you to come, right as the plane rises in the air." I stepped close to her, giving us no space between each other.

Erotic heat radiated from her sexy frame. "That sounds like a good plan."

"Before you'll know it, we'll be in Prague."

"But that's not Russia."

"We have things to do there."

"What?"

"That is not important." I zipped down her leather jacket. "This is what's important."

Asking no more questions, she watched me undress her. With each item, I took my time. The material of her clothes didn't compare to the softness of her skin. I was crazy to have her flesh beneath my fingers.

Chatter ensued beyond the door as the rest of our crew getting into their seats. Things slammed shut or banged against each other. It could've been the grew loading the luggage. I didn't care.

Emily stood before me like a present begging to be unwrapped and cherished.

Most of her clothes dropped to the floor. I let Emily keep her bra and panties on. They were black lace and silk—perfect and ready to be ripped off.

Grunting, I whispered, "My little *mysh*."

She remained still. Sweet patience decorated her face, yet hot desire blazed within in her eyes.

"You want this cock?"

Her voice came out as a whisper. "Yes."

"Hmmm." I licked my lips. "Today, I decided that I want to own your smiles."

She widened her eyes.

"I didn't like you smiling at Maxwell, before we got on the plane." I shrugged. "But, I understand your relationship with him, so I. . ."

How could I explain without scaring her?

She finished the sentence for me. "So, you didn't roar."

Clever wording.

My cock hardened. "Yes. So, I didn't roar."

"I don't want to make you roar, but. . ." She looked unsure of what to say next.

I guessed. "But, you won't be caged?"

"I won't."

The pilot must've turned the engine on because the floor vibrated under my feet.

"I understand, Emily."

She sighed in relief.

"But."

She raised her eyebrows.

"But, what if the cage was around the globe?" I leaned my head to the side. "Wouldn't you feel less trapped?"

Her expression shifted to neutral. "That hypothetical scares me. I would rather you just fuck me, instead of ask those questions."

"Hmmm." I stepped close to her. Barely an inch lay between us. Through the black bra, her hard nipples sat on top of her perky breasts. Her body screamed a promise of delicious passion, and I couldn't wait to feast. It took everything in me to not move so fast and stuff my cock into right there.

I touched her hips and slipped my hands along her curvy frame.

Sighing, she closed her eyes as I tip toed my fingers up to her breasts. "Kaz."

Unable to keep myself calm after she whispered that name, I devoured Emily's mouth, and carried her to the bed. "I need to be inside you."

"Please." Her hands went to my shirt and yanked at the buttons, snatching the thread from them. I hurried out of my jacket right as she tore away the rest of my shirt. "Valentina is going to lose it, when she sees that newly tailored shirt in pieces."

"You started it."

I raised my eyebrows. "When?"

"You ripped away my bra with your teeth."

"I did?"

"You did."

"Hmmm. Was it like this?" I lowered down to her cleavage. Moaning, she arched her breasts up to meet my mouth. It took no time to capture the center of the bra with my teeth and tear it away. Those lovely mounts jiggled free from the binding black lace, exposing everything to me. Her hard nipples pointed my way. A second later and my mouth was on her, lapping and licking.

Moaning, she gripped the sheets on the bed.

Once I'd gotten a taste of her, I couldn't hold myself back anymore.

"Oh, *mysh*." I shifted from her breasts to that lovely mouth. "

My body blared with need. I reached between us, undid my pants, and took out my cock. The whole time, my mouth remained on hers. I didn't break our kiss as I pushed her panties to the side.

How did I live this long without fucking her?

Sex with her was like breathing, and I was desperate to inhale and exhale every inch of her body. Without thinking, I thrust deep my cock deep inside her, hard and fast, swallowing her sexy moans with my kisses.

Her pussy was soaking wet. I slid in and out of her with ease. She must've been dripping the entire time we'd been talking. I gripped Emily unable to be as gentle as before. All I could do was feed my desire and pound deep into her. And I did. Holding her in place, I gaver her every thick inch of me, pumping and thrusting. With every stroke, she shrieked so loud everyone else on the plane must've heard.

"Kaz."

"Say it again."

She gripped my shoulders. "Kaz."

My thrusting shifted to longer, slower shoves. I leaned back a little to watch her breasts bounce as I fucked her. "Look at what I'm doing to you."

She lifted her head and directed her gaze to where I pierced her. My cock slipped in and out of that wet pussy. The very view had me close to cuming all over her.

It was in that moment that I realized I wore no condom.

"Fuck." I slipped out of her. "We forgot."

"What?" An exasperated breath left her lips. "Forgot what?"

"The condom."

She hit my chest. "I don't care. Just fuck me."

"Suddenly, you don't care?" I grinned and pressed the throbbing point at her opening. "Hmmm. I do like my cock covered with you."

"Fuck me hard, Kaz." She moved one hand to where we were joined, touching my cock as it met her opening. "Please. Don't make me beg."

My body burned with insanity. Every cell yearned to have us back inside of her. But she didn't need to know how much she could tame me.

"I think I would love to hear you beg."

She pouted. The expression looked so foreign on her.

I rubbed the tip along the opening. "Play with your clit."

With pleading eyes, she moved her hand higher and toyed with that button. Hunger ripped from her throat.

"Oh, yes. Let me watch you get off." I pushed my cock into that sweet pussy, trying to tease her. But it was a lackluster approach. I couldn't even stop myself as I slipped in and out of her. And then she forgot her clit as she took my pounding, groaning with desire as I stuffed her with me.

I leaned down, sucked her nipple into my mouth, and then grazed the sensitive point with my teeth. The move sent both of us on edge. At this pace, I'd be damn close to spilling cum all over her.

I held her still and thrust deeply, adjusting my angle. She went crazy, putting her arms up behind her and grabbing the edge of the bed as I drove into her.

"Oh, Kaz. Don't stop."

"If you didn't want to be caged, you should've never gave me this pussy." I reached down and rubbed her throbbing clit, giving her the pressure, she needed. With my cock encased in that lush heat, I wouldn't last much longer. I pinched her nipple with my other hand, rocking into her wet creamy center.

Her breaths shifted to pants and her pussy clenched around my cock, milking the fuck out of me. "I'm close."

"Oh, cum for me, Emily. Show me how much you love this cock."

"Oh!"

I thrust in hard, wanting us to orgasm together. "You're so wet, but I'm going to make you even more messy."

She groaned.

"Tell me you want this cum inside of you."

"Fill me." Her body trembled under mine.

I tenderly pinch her clit, pushing her further over the edge. And then her body tensed against mine.

"Oh, Kaz," she screamed as her orgasm takes her.

She was beautiful—all ragged breaths and bucking hips. And then I fell into my own orgasm, rocking into her like a madman. Unable to control my cock or body.

Fuck! You're mine, Emily. All fucking mine.

I filled her up with me, soaking that warm pussy and dripping all over her. And there was no worry about making her pregnant or anything else. These past days had proven that our lives were out of control, but definitely meant to be linked together.

But for how long? And why am I even thinking about this?

Coming down from her orgasm, she fell back into the bed. "Oh my God."

I glanced at the opened window. We were moving, and barely a minute or so from taking off.

Oblivious, she rode the aftershocks of pleasure, and all I wanted to do was take care of her.

Completely out of character, I rose from the bed, went into the bathroom, and grabbed a warm cloth. When I returned, she lay on her side, close to falling asleep.

Her legs were still open. My cum shimmered on her entrance.

I'm cleaning her pussy of me. She has no idea how much I'm under her control. She can't ever know. In fact, no one could ever know.

I wiped away the mess I'd made of her lovely pussy, whispering my vow to come back and lick her later. I doubted Emily heard me as she fell asleep.

Get some rest. We have ten hours on this plane, and I plan on using them.

I watched her sleep unsure of what to do with myself. Any other time, I would've sent the woman I'd fucked on her way. There would've been no reason for her to remain in my bed. Once I'd got some pussy, I was done.

But with Emily, there would be no done. At least no time in this future.

What is she doing to me?

I frowned as I lay down next to her.

Yawning, she snuggled up against me.

I wrapped my arms around her and closed my eyes. "What will I do with you, little *mysh*."

The plane's engine rumbled harder as it lifted us in the air, causing the bed to vibrate under its power. Emily trembled against me, but never woke up.

You're missing your first take off. Don't worry, mysh, there will be other flights and other times I fuck you to sleep.

As if she heard my thoughts through her dreams, she rolled over to me. I tightened my hold around her. Our warm bodies molded together—breasts to chest. Arms and legs entangled. Scents mingled with the silk of the sheets.

A minute later, the plane roared even more and lifted us higher into the sky. Emily trembled a little. Next came soft snores from her parted lips and the sound of her heartbeats thumping against mine.

What will become of us? What will happen to the mouse and the lion?